The shadow warrior appeared as if from nowhere . . .

The two swords met, joined, one as real as the other.

Sparks from the striking blades kept time with the sound of their meeting. Back and forth the two figures moved, cutting, then passing through. Every move had a countermove. Every step a counterstep.

The katana became an extension of her arms. Iroshi felt the friction as it sliced the air, a faint hum spreading from sword tip to toes. Meet the blade. Defend. Attack. Keep moving. Forever . . .

"FLASHING BLADES, BODILESS ALIENS, AND DEADLY
ninja, all cleanly welded into slam-bang space
opera. Osborne is a welcome addition
to the small group of authors
who write knowledgeably
about martial arts."
—STEVE PERRY

The Glaive

Osborne

IROSHI

CARY OSBORNE

ACE BOOKS, NEW YORK

This book is an Ace original edition,
and has never been previously published.

IROSHI

An Ace Book / published by arrangement with the author

PRINTING HISTORY
Ace edition / November 1995

All rights reserved.
Copyright © 1995 by Cary Osborne.
Cover art by Jean-François Podevin.
This book may not be reproduced in whole or in part,
by mimeograph or any other means, without permission.
For information address: The Berkley Publishing Group,
200 Madison Avenue, New York, NY 10016.

ISBN: 0-441-00130-0

ACE®
Ace Books are published by The Berkley Publishing Group,
200 Madison Avenue, New York, NY 10016.
ACE and the "A" design are trademarks
belonging to Charter Communications, Inc.

PRINTED IN THE UNITED STATES OF AMERICA

10 9 8 7 6 5 4 3 2 1

PART I

1

Ronin

Her footsteps echoed through the nearly empty terminal as Iroshi approached the customs counter. The agent leered as she lifted two bags onto the counter for inspection. The leer disappeared when he saw the swords tucked neatly in the first case. Without opening the second, he quickly tagged each and pushed them toward her.

Being a ronin did have its advantages, a fact proven on several worlds by people who had probably never seen one in person before she arrived. There were only a few roaming among the colonies, but even in a remote, failing one like this, the legends of such warriors were always present.

The books described this as a desolate planet called Rune because of ancient writings found everywhere, engraved on rocks and ruins of buildings. The original survey had taken place more than thirty-five years ago, and the writings had never been translated. Now the newest civilization trying to make its mark here was dying.

The ancient, alien civilization could provide a fascinating study, but that was not why she came. Not that she had any more idea of what had drawn her to Rune than what had drawn her to twelve other worlds. The knowing where to go was an instinctive thing and still a mystery to her. Each place had provided a lesson in kendo, the "way of the sword," which she hoped drew her closer to the void. At best they were only stepping stones toward that goal and the unknown quest.

The street was dusty in the heat of the sun. She shaded

3

her eyes to see the poor excuse of a hotel down on the left side. That was her immediate goal.

"Is there a constable here?" she asked the desk clerk as she signed the old-fashioned register.

"Yeah. Out the door, turn left. On this side of the street." He pushed the credit disc into the slot, and handed it back with a key disc when the proper message appeared on the monitor.

The room was on the second floor. She tossed the bags on the bed, then washed up. No running water here; a pitcher of water and a basin sufficed on arid planets. She dried her face on the towel and dumped the water into the recycler. It began dripping back into the pitcher almost at once.

No need to unpack everything, since her stay would only be one or two nights. She did take out the shinai, the bamboo sword, and thrust it through her belt. Used with precision, it could stand up against any weapon except a gun, but for now it served as a symbol of training and skill and as a warning to the men of the town. Some, like the customs clerk, had exhibited an improper interest. The looks on the faces in the lobby as she passed back through showed that the point was well taken.

The constable was not in his office, but she had barely seated herself in the uncomfortable plastic chair when he came in. He looked her up and down, gaze resting on the shinai for a moment.

"Heard you were in town. . . . Iroshi, isn't it?"

He rounded the rusty metal desk and sat in the chair opposite her. The screech as it took his weight grated against her ears. Outwardly, she gave no sign of hearing it or his calling her by name. The desk clerk might have told him, or it was possible that word was sent ahead by Constable Wimer back on Byron.

She looked across the desk at him, deliberately returning the appraisal before she spoke.

"I will be in your town a couple of nights at most. What

I'm looking for is a completely isolated place where I can stay for a time."

He laughed as if she had made a dumb joke.

"Most of this planet's like that."

"I need someplace that has water. I understand there are several areas of ruins."

He nodded.

"Are any of them suitable?"

"No water at any of them. There isn't much water out there, anywhere. Most of the nearest ruins are used by prospectors. Don't know if there's anyone beyond the temple."

"The temple?" Awareness woke, skittered along her nerves.

"Yeah. No one goes near it. A lot of people believe it's haunted. Ain't never been there myself. Don't know if there's any water. Your best bet would be to go farther out. Probably aren't any prospectors out that far anymore."

"What direction?"

"East. About six hundred klicks to the temple."

"And in the other direction?"

"West of here? A few small ruins. More prospectors but not much else. It's less a wasteland than east. That's why it's more populated."

He leaned back in his screeching chair, laced his fingers behind his head.

"Where can I get supplies?" she asked.

"There's a store across from the hotel. They can fix you up. You got transportation?"

"Yes. I made arrangements at the terminal before I arrived." She turned toward the door.

"There's one thing you should keep in mind."

Iroshi turned back, noting that his listless posture and drawl had sharpened somewhat, as if he had been putting on an act for the tourist.

"There aren't many women on Rune anymore. And the men who are left haven't any money. Only the raunchy ones are left. Some might want you. Some might want whatever else you have of value." He motioned toward the shinai. "That stick sword won't protect you from a gun. In spite of your reputation."

So, word had come, probably from Byron.

"I know, Constable . . ."

"Mitchell."

"Thank you, Constable Mitchell, for the warning and the information."

She left the office, headed for the store. It was her habit to be ready to leave at a moment's notice, a habit often reinforced by necessity. Purchases were made quickly: food, medical supplies, lanterns, and, most important, water and portable recycler. She had brought a sleeping bag and personal items.

It was almost dark by the time everything was sorted, bundled, and stacked in the room. She made her way down to the hotel dining room, a large bare chamber, and ordered a light dinner. The food was surprisingly good, although plain and preprocessed.

The four other diners, all sitting at separate tables, cast sidelong glances but left her alone. She was accustomed to being stared at and knowing she, or her adventures, were the topic of conversation. Eventually someone always tried to start a conversation, at the least spurred by curiosity. It usually took a little longer for anyone to work up courage or be goaded into challenging her. Before that happened, she should be gone.

The presence of the shinai had brought about a marked decrease in overt interest. No one spoke to her unless she spoke first. The lack of any aggressiveness roused her curiosity, but she shrugged mentally, attributing their attitudes to the slow death of the colony and the dimming hopes for fortunes in what mining might be left. Still, it would warrant attention later if time allowed.

Rune, she had read, was the last and outermost of the colonies. Most of the worlds, like her home planet of

Siebeling, were opened up for the mining of precious metals, all of which were depleted on Earth. These minerals were the main source of income for the central government, such as it was, which received payment for mining rights and twenty-five percent of all profits. This control was becoming the only base of power for the government as the companies grew stronger, assuming leadership in many areas, dividing the worlds among themselves, as the number of colonized planets increased.

Early tests on Rune had indicated the possibility of large amounts of those metals. Company towns followed the reports, dotting the surface of the planet, populated by miners full of hope and empty of pocket, as was usual with many of their kind. The company miners left with hope gone too, as the promise of fortune turned to sand, and their employers moved them to more lucrative locations. Only two towns still operated; this one, Spencer, and Logan, supplying the diehard and desperate independent prospectors, either still dreaming of finding a fortune or unable to pay for passage off-planet.

Spencer had the only operating space terminal. The law said that the companies must keep at least one terminal going until the colony was issued its official death pronouncement. It was one of the few laws religiously observed even though the tattered edges of the unnamed empire steadily unraveled.

She sighed, a little sigh. Philosophizing about it was a waste of time, and the demise of the loosely knit empire of colonies and companies was of little personal interest. There were more important things to consider.

The possibility of being left alone in the desert while everyone else came to their senses and evacuated Rune was one. However, the chances of that happening anytime soon were small, and meeting the constable, letting him know she was on-planet, was a clause in a personal insurance policy against it. It took a long time to dismantle a colony.

Then, the compulsion to be here was too great to let such fears deter her.

Such compulsions were what pushed her forward. Some had yielded small results, while others had been very rewarding. Rewarding enough to keep following them in the hope that one, somewhere, might equal those she had found on Earth.

Iroshi paid for the meal and went up to the room. In spite of all logic, the general attitude of the men and the comments of the constable had created an undercurrent of disquiet. She decided to sleep on the floor in the corner that could not be seen from either the door or window. Before lying down on the sleeping bag, she messed up the bedcovers, shaping them with the pillows to give the appearance of a reclining body.

Only a few hours passed when she woke. It was still dark outside and inside. Someone was in the room, had awakened her with a noise or with his presence alone. She listened with controlled breathing, until her ears rang with the black silence. He was being very cautious. A slight creak in a joint in the floor came from the other side of the bed near the door. Her eyes, drawn by the noise, made out a darker figure, given visibility by a moment of motion.

Very slowly, Iroshi slipped the pistol from under the edge of the sleeping bag. There was not room enough in the small space for proper use of the sword, nor was the intruder worthy of her skills. She fired just as the figure attacked the form on the bed. He yelled in pain and a dull thump followed. She cursed softly, knowing instinctively that it had not been a clean hit.

She rose to her knees for a second shot. The door creaked open and watery light sneaked in from the hall. She stood but could not see him as he stayed low to the floor, using the bed between them to shield his movements. A quick shot flared into the hall, burning the plastiwood of the wall as he bolted through the opening. By the time she reached the hall he was gone, with too many possible routes for pursuit. She had never seen his features, so she could not even identify him.

Silently she dressed and slipped out of the hotel into the early morning coolness. It was time to leave, to find her way into the desert where she could train and meditate in peace.

The rented sand buggy sat where it had the day before. She ran her hands over its surface, its balloon tires, under the hood, touching much of the engine, letting her fingers sense the kinds of things her eyes could not see even in daylight. This was a part of her not learned through kendo, Zen, or any other training, a natural talent honed by practice and necessity.

The machine was worn; many parts would not stand much more stress. The toolbox contained some replacement parts, in good condition, as well as tools. At last she was satisfied. With the parts and tools, it would get her where she wanted to go and back. As a little added insurance she scrounged an extra cylinder of fuel, hydrogen on this planet, and put it in the back. The fuel was refined from ice at the southern pole. Water, the only by-product, was collected for reuse. All colony worlds had one kind of native fuel or another. If not, they were judged too expensive to bother with.

Iroshi returned to the hotel, gathered up her gear as quietly as possible, and returned to the buggy. She got everything loaded, apparently without attracting attention, and turned the motor on. It was loud. Too loud to escape town without notice. She shoved it in gear and moved down the street following the route she had memorized earlier that day. Too soon the temperature rose and she had to stop, let the engine cool. The old machine was never meant to run at high speed for long.

While it cooled, she listened for any pursuit, felt for any nearby presence. Nothing or no one came along the road, but she was relieved when the readout on the gauge indicated it was safe to restart the buggy. The motor roared through the darkness, wheels on one side or the other leaving the road often, until she was far enough from Spencer that it seemed safe to turn on the headlamps.

It was nearly noon, and hot under the canopy, when she reached what could only be the area of the temple. The distance was about right: 626 klicks on the odometer. The ruined buildings danced in the heat-shimmer a mile or so to the left. Even at that distance, they had the look and feel of a special place.

She turned from the road toward her intended destination, since the constable's mention of them had struck a chord within her. That chord grew louder the closer she got, enveloping her, summoning memories. Memories of another time when she arrived at another place both strange and familiar like this one. Memories of Mushimo and Crowell, six years past, when she was still Laicy Campbell.

2

An Old Samurai

It was her first time on Earth, but she felt as if she knew exactly where she was going. Crowell's directions had been vague, at best, since he had not been in Tokyo in a very long time himself. From his description, things had changed considerably. Thank goodness the driver seemed to recognize the name.

As they moved easily through the city, she was struck by the small number of people and vehicles. Most cities on Siebeling were ten times more crowded than this. Of course, overpopulation had been the impetus for man's gradual dispersal to the stars, beginning over four centuries ago. Either the exodus had continued for a very long time, perhaps was still going on, or Terrans had learned other ways to handle the problem.

The road wound through the city, to its outskirts, and into the countryside for several miles. Instinct told her they had arrived just as the driver guided the car onto the grass alongside the road. She stepped out and looked around. It was the middle of nowhere. No side roads as far as one could see in either direction. Her attention was drawn to the woods a short distance away. Just at their edge stood a man, leaning on a staff, staring at her.

"Hello," she yelled. "Can you give me directions?"

"No," he answered simply.

"But I'm trying to find a Mr. Mushimo. I think . . ."

"I have been waiting for you."

She stared in disbelief.

"Are *you* Mr. Mushimo?"

He bowed, then moved toward her. As soon as he was within an arm's length, he bowed again. She reciprocated, feeling foolish. It was a common enough courtesy inside the dojo, part of the kendo tradition, but was the only place and time Laicy had ever done so.

His appearance was startling. She had pictured an old man, one who had once possessed great strength, now bowed with the weight of many battles. In her mind's eye he was reticent, unwilling to speak of past exploits, further indication of the great warrior Crowell had described.

Before her, however, was a tall, lean man with a gay twinkle in his eye. He leaned on the long staff, but seemingly more out of habit than need.

"I'm Laicy Campbell. But if you knew I was coming, you must know my name."

"Of course. Crowell told me you would be arriving and your name. That is why I was waiting there." He pointed toward the spot at the edge of the woods where she had first seen him.

"Your bags?"

"Oh, yes."

The driver had set them on the ground while they were talking and now he waited for his money. It was a moment before Laicy realized that.

"Oh," she said again as both men looked at her. She fumbled in her wallet.

"How much?"

"Seventeen credits."

She pulled out several bits of paper and handed them over. He looked at them with distaste.

"Don't you have a credit disc?"

"No, I'm afraid not." She had no idea what he was talking about. "All I have are those bills. Isn't it any good?"

He sighed in disgust, looked about to reply with harsh words.

"On with you now," Mr. Mushimo said. "Paper credits are still good."

He picked up one of her large bags.

"I will carry this one. Can you manage the others?"

She nodded, watched him move back toward the woods. The bag he chose was the heaviest—it held her swords and most of the other weapons she had brought with her—but he carried it easily. Hastily, she picked up the other large bag, the smaller one already slung over her shoulder, and moved off after him. The taxi pulled away, but she didn't look back.

"The walk to my home and the dojo, the school, is not long. The dojo is where you will train."

She could only mutter a reply. The path through the woods sloped steeply downward. It took total concentration on her feet to keep them from becoming entangled in briers or roots. Once they reached the bottom, the way led immediately back up another hill. From the summit she could see a flat space cut by a rocky stream. A group of low buildings, surrounded by a high fence, appeared in the woods in the distance. The water in the stream was icy when she waded the few steps. As she neared the gate, a middle-aged man came running from the dojo and took the bags, fussing all the time in a strange language she assumed to be Japanese. She smiled at his scolding tone, and looked at her guide to see him smiling too.

"Akiro will show you to your room. We will talk at dinner."

Mushimo bowed and moved away. She returned the bow, again feeling awkward, then rushed after the still-scolding servant before he moved out of sight.

The room was spacious and airy with a large, comfortable mattress lying on the floor. As if that wasn't strange enough, the only place to wash up was a bowl and a pitcher of water on a small wooden stand. Even on Siebeling, as out of the mainstream as it was, there were ordinary showers and bathrooms in each house. She pulled off pants and shirt, washed up as best she could, then lay down on the mattress in her underwear. Everything was going smoothly enough, although the first meeting with Mushimo had turned out rather oddly.

Crowell had often talked about his old master, saying that he was the best kendo teacher still living, as far as he knew. Such statements were usually colored by personal feelings as much as truth, but she trusted Crowell's opinion. He had been her teacher for nearly eight years, during which time a mutual respect, even fondness, had grown. He had praised her skills and dedication, in the end said he had taught her everything he could. He wanted her to progress, to learn what only his old master could teach.

Her mother had assumed a sad expression when told her daughter was to leave, but the woman's relief was obvious. It meant that only two children, James and David, would be left to feed and care for. Crowell put up the credits for the trip, so there was no expense for her. Laicy was the eldest, knew her mother loved her, and tried to understand. But it hurt.

A knock on the door snapped her from her reverie.

"Yes?" she called.

"Dinner is ready in the garden, miss," a male voice said.

Dinner? She had eaten breakfast on the liner just a short time before planetfall.

"Thank you. I'll only be a moment."

She peeked through the blinds in time to see the old servant withdrawing.

Dressing quickly, she walked out onto the veranda, thinking that she would probably have to walk the full perimeter of the building to locate the garden. To the right was as good a start as any.

"This way, miss."

She wheeled around to see the man beckoning in the opposite direction. She would have sworn that he had walked away. As she fell in behind him she asked, "What is your name?"

"Akiro."

"Oh, yes."

Mushimo sat at the table, on a cushion on the ground. *Another strange custom,* she thought, seating herself opposite him.

He bowed his head and she responded. It was getting easier.

"Is it just the two of us?"

"Yes. You are the only student at present. There are not many these days. Partly because there is little regard for the old ways. Young people cannot seem to dedicate themselves to anything except the making of money or reputation. Partly because I am getting too old. I usually accept only those who have shown great promise and who are recommended by old students of mine. Like Crowell."

As he talked she relaxed, the tension soothed away by the kindness in his voice.

"He didn't tell me much about you."

"And you came anyway."

It was a statement, yet there was the expectation of an answer.

"Yes. I trust him and . . ." She paused. It was not her way to tell innermost thoughts or feelings even to a good friend. And this was still a stranger sitting across the table.

"And . . ." he prompted, looking solemnly into her eyes. "He told me very little about you also."

She held that gaze a moment, then looked away.

"Except that you are a superb swordswoman," he continued.

"I want to be the best I can be. It's as simple as that."

"Not so simple, I think."

For a time they concentrated on the food. Many of the dishes were very good, but few were familiar. It was a simple pleasure to have real food again after three weeks of preprocessed food on the liner, and she found her appetite quickened. He told her the name of each dish as she sampled it. The one she liked most was a hot drink he called tea.

Somehow she went from such safe bits of conversation

to talking about her life on Siebeling. The planet was a long-established mining colony, and her parents were second-generation residents. Jonathon Campbell had abandoned the family in a nameless mining town to go into space on a freighter, leaving a wife and three children to fend for themselves. Her mother had supported Laicy and the two boys with various jobs in the mines. For extra money she had also taken in laundry. The town swarmed with unattached men who did not want to wash shirts and sheets when they were off duty.

Laicy went to school, and helped with the washing. There were two big machines set up in the shed and one oversized dryer. She could load, unload, and fold six loads in two hours. When she was old enough, she got a job as a waitress in the company food service.

Five years ago, when she was twelve, she had met and started classes with Robert Crowell. After that, all she cared about was kendo. The mental and physical discipline appealed at first as a way to rise above a mere existence. Soon it became an end in itself. She was born to it. Her mother hadn't cared, so long as she continued to help with the laundry and the cost of the classes came out of what Laicy made for herself.

When Crowell announced a few months ago that there was nothing more he could teach her, the only thing left to do was to practice. Religiously. And reread and meditate on the words of the old masters.

She visited his dojo every day to practice with the mechanical spar or another student when possible. Occasionally Crowell could give her some time. He didn't charge her as he did others, knowing she could not afford full price for the time, and the cost of a spar was certainly out of reach.

Crowell did not tell her that he had contacted his old teacher back on Earth to see if he would take one more student. He waited until Mushimo's consent arrived.

Her apprehensions about leaving what was familiar were

small compared with those of meeting the towering master (Mushimo smiled at that). But she would have left at once if it were not for the usual red tape: off-planet clearances, releases from her mother, credits to be transferred to her, then to the transport company, and on interminably.

To make matters worse, Earth, although the seat of government, was a secondary destination and it took extra time to find a starliner making a stop there. Laicy practiced constantly, beating at the hours and days with her swords, until at last the day of departure came.

Saying goodbye to Crowell was difficult. He was a true friend. Saying goodbye to her brothers and mother was hard for other reasons.

Emotion made her tongue-tied at that point, bringing her narrative to a close.

"I'm afraid I've talked too much," she apologized.

Given a moment to think about it, she grew embarrassed at how much she had told him.

"No more than I encouraged you to," he returned. "That was the first test."

"Test? Did I fail?"

"It was not a question of passing or failing, although you acted as I would have wanted. It was a multifaceted test; not the least part was to see if you instinctively trust me. You do, or you would not have told me so much. Your trust probably originates from Crowell's teaching. That gives us a basis on which to begin working. Tomorrow, we will see how well he has done in other areas."

The next day, true to his word, he put her through all the exercises she had ever learned, then showed her a few new ones. His stamina was a wonder to her as she sat exhausted at the dinner table in the evening. Over the next few months, he would drill into her, and she would learn it was true, that he was not necessarily stronger than she. It was just that he had practiced and taught so many years and had learned how to never put more energy into a movement than was necessary. With this knowledge he conserved his strength, while she wasted much of hers. But she would learn.

For the first week they concentrated on the physical side of the training alone. The second week he introduced her to real books, copies of writings by some of the ancient masters, so different from the book tapes to which she was accustomed. Her time was then divided between reading and practicing.

She treasured the books, the feel of them as much as their contents. She had never found in the tapes works as old as some of these books. If Mushimo had not chided, she would have spent more time turning pages than swinging a blade. He demanded a balanced education.

" 'Pen and sword in accord,' " he quoted one day. "An old Japanese saying."

"I don't understand," she said.

"Have you never heard then, 'The pen is mightier than the sword'?"

She shook her head. He shrugged ancient shoulders and wandered away, mumbling something about colonials and youth.

Her favorite book was *A Book of Five Rings* by Miyamoto Musashi, a sixteenth-century samurai warrior. He was a ronin, a wandering warrior with no war to fight and no lord to serve with his sword. Some called him a beast, barely human. Legend said that he had won sixty personal combats before he was twenty-nine, many of them with wooden sword against steel blade. She envied his prowess, although occasionally she doubted the truth of some of the fantastic tales written about him. His philosophy of strategy was intriguing but seemed beyond her understanding. "The Book of the Void," the final chapter, and the shortest one, was the most puzzling.

Mushimo taught her from the books in the mornings. Afternoons she practiced, usually with the shinai, sometimes against the spar, an automated practice dummy that could hurt but not kill. Sometimes Mushimo introduced her to the finer points of the art, not always in a gentle manner.

He insisted that she also practice with other weapons—halberd or glaive, sickle, nun chaku, and others—as well as learning to use her own body as a weapon.

"A warrior should never be without a weapon," he said over and over.

The sword would always be the weapon of greatest skill, more natural to her, wielded with a grace he openly admired.

At last one morning he began teaching from *A Book of Five Rings*. She was ecstatic that at last Musashi's words would be made clear. When midday came, however, she concluded that it was beyond her.

"I just don't understand. Even after your explanation."

"Then why are you drawn so strongly to his words?"

"I have no idea. There is something in his philosophy which I sense is important to me, a message that I am somehow missing."

"You will find it," he said and chuckled. "Sometimes, Laicy, working for the knowledge is part of the lesson. Now shoo!"

She scrambled off to meditate in her favorite corner of the garden. Nearly thirty-five minutes of the hour were gone when sharp sounds intruded, bringing her back to the present space/time. It was the sound of swordplay, but not in practice. There was anger.

She came to her feet, moving through a gate in the wall out into the woods, around to the front of the complex. Just inside the gate Mushimo matched swords with two men clothed completely in black except for their eyes. She watched in fascination for a short time as the three moved in and out of view inside the fence.

The initial reaction was one of shock at seeing two real ninja warriors. The sect was extinct, or so the books said. Inside, the suspicion grew that this was some kind of test, and she decided to observe a while longer—until she noticed two more ninja in the shadow of the gate moving closer to the combatants from behind Mushimo. He was handling the two easily, but four against one were not fair odds.

Keeping to cover of trees and bushes, Laicy approached the gate unseen, and slipped within just in time to put herself between a black-clad enemy and his intended victim. He wielded the shorter sword of the ninja. It would take every bit of skill she had to keep her shinai from being cut to pieces.

Parrying the first cut, she turned the shinai so that the blow was a glancing one. Hoping to surprise him, she attacked quickly, swinging repeatedly so that he had no time to retaliate. He stumbled back, tripped over a root. She beat at him, keeping him off balance, and he fell. Somehow he kept hold of the sword. Even so, she managed to catch him on the left shoulder; his guard dropped slightly, and she knocked him unconscious with a blow on the side of the head.

An instant later, a searing pain in her right side paralyzed her. She stumbled forward, right hand moving to press against the wound. She twisted left, regained her balance, saw both the attacker and Akiro. The servant approached the ninja from behind, sword in hand. His demeanor was confident, his movements precise. Laicy felt a momentary surprise seeing him as a warrior for the first time.

She glanced down at the first opponent, lying unconscious on the ground. The second attacked again. Through the pain in her side, she wondered why he took so long.

Akiro, too, moved slowly, drawing closer. She assumed a combat stance, keeping the ninja's attention. Akiro struck. Blood spurted from the side of the man's neck. Laicy slipped to her knees and did not see him fall. Akiro looked toward her, then glanced back at his master, whom she could not see, for a bush was in her line of sight. Akiro was apparently satisfied that Mushimo was managing without him. He came to her, helped her to unsteady feet, supporting her as she swayed slightly.

The sound of swords suddenly stopped. There was a grunt of pain as servant and student rounded the bush just in time to see the last of the attackers collapse.

Mushimo stood poised above his fallen enemy for some time, sword held upright in both hands and to his right. In spite of her confusion and pain, she felt amazement at how a man his age could fight so well. She was at least fifty years younger and had found it impossible to handle two opponents, while he had dispatched two with no help and no apparent wounds.

Blood seeped through her fingers, ran down her side. Both her head and stomach swam. She leaned more heavily on Akiro, forcing him to ease her to the grass. Mushimo appeared over her, his eyes full of concern.

"We must get her to her room," he said to Akiro.

All of her floated. Lights flashed, went dark. No sound or movement except for the world turning beneath her. Dreams. Memories.

Faces hovered within sight. On the third day she awoke, vision clear, feeling hungry and thirsty.

Akiro and three other servants, who had only been shadows before, fed her, washed her, and otherwise fussed over her. They coaxed her to wellness. When she at last became totally aware, Mushimo came to sit beside her twice a day. In the mornings he read to her, and in the afternoons they talked, sometimes about her, more often about philosophy or martial arts. One afternoon she finally asked what she had hoped he would volunteer.

"Who were those men who attacked you?"

He looked away and remained silent for a very long time.

"They were ninja, students of an old enemy."

"I thought there were no more ninja."

"Very few. Here on Earth and a few scattered among the

colonies. They are not quite the same as the ones you read about in the old books."

"Was their attack a surprise?"

"Yes. The feud has lain dormant many years. I would not have accepted another student had I thought there was any danger."

Another prolonged silence held. She sensed there was more to the story than his words said.

"You handled yourself well," he added.

"Frankly, I never expected to be in a fight with someone. Not a real swordfight. Looked at logically, it seems so archaic. I've learned to use the sword because it's something I'm good at. Kendo and Zen give me the physical and mental discipline I need. But . . . I mean . . . We have laser pistols and sonic cannon and other more sophisticated, modern, and deadly weapons."

"As you saw for yourself, swords are still used. There are people who will only fight in traditional ways. Planets where all kinds of guns are banned for various reasons, not the least being safety. A gun is more likely to pierce the walls of a habitat. In some places, hand weapons are a matter of honor. On the other hand, swords and knives are the preferred weapons of assassination.

"You will not leave here without training in the use of the more modern weapons. But it is not a difficult thing to learn. It takes longer to learn the art of the sword.

"For now, you must rest, get your strength back."

He made good on his promise. Not long after her full recovery, training in all sizes and shapes of guns began. It was not Mushimo who taught her these skills, but Akiro, who had already revealed his ability with the sword. His skill with a laser rifle was also an art.

The days passed as they had before the spasm of excitement. She trained every day, studied the books and meditated, and still found much of the philosophy not quite understandable. She decided that, being too far from their time, she would never grasp even the basics. She took satisfaction in the honing of her skills with the sword and other weapons to the point of perfection. The truth of her ability was confirmed in her teacher's eyes.

One morning she joined Mushimo in the garden for breakfast as usual. Laicy could no longer imagine eating anywhere else, except when they were kept inside by bad weather. Even on cold days, if the sun was shining, they ate outside.

For some reason, the memory of the first time they had eaten together at that table flooded her mind. But it was more than simple memory. Feelings, doubts of that time, changed with her increased skills. She could feel it deep within, had seen without realizing the changes in the mirror.

Mushimo spoke, bringing her attention to the moment.

"Akiro, bring Laicy's weapons from her room."

She was curious but said nothing.

Akiro returned and offered the bundles to his master. Mushimo motioned to Laicy, and the servant laid them in front of her. The shinai, which she used every day, lay on top of the bundle. She lifted it, placed it in front of Mushimo, and unwrapped the cloth. A small bokken, or lightweight wooden sword, and a sturdier wooden sword she laid beside the shinai. Then the companion sword, the wakizashi, in its sheath, a gift from Crowell.

Four swords in all. She reached toward the second bundle of smaller weapons. Mushimo picked up the wakizashi, watched the sun reflect from the steel blade as he drew it from the sheath.

"Where is your long sword, your katana?"

"I have not earned one yet. I am not a warrior. I cannot even carry the companion sword."

Her puzzlement increased. He must know that.

"But you must learn to use one. Come with me."

He led the way into the house, into the weapons room, which she had seen once but never entered. Wooden racks stood against each wall; several more stood randomly throughout the room. Racks stacked with halberds, spears, knives, and weapons she had never seen the likes of before. And swords. Long swords, companion swords, even a few of utterly alien design. Mushimo had told her that all the swords were ancient, a few over a thousand years old, and the collection was priceless. He waved his hand in a half circle.

"Choose a sword, Laicy."

She looked again at the racks, then at him.

"I cannot. Each deserves a better hand than mine," she heard herself say. "They are much too valuable. And too fine."

"Your hand is good and will be better. As your teacher I tell you: choose."

She experienced the uneasy feeling again. More lay behind the offer than she could understand, or even guess. She turned. There were so many. How to choose just one, just the *right* one? She moved from rack to rack, her mind becoming confused as if many voices whispered instructions. Confusion grew as she moved farther into the room. Once she glanced back at Mushimo, hoping for his assistance. His face remained completely immobile.

She stopped in front of a rack. The voices faded. Twelve swords lay horizontally in their places. The fourth one from the top held her. She reached up and lifted it out to cradle it across her palms. The burnished outer surface of the sheath spiraled like a twisted rope. Slowly, she gripped the handle, then slid the slightly curved blade free. It was magnificent in its simplicity.

A stylized dragon, carved into the steel, stretched along one-third the length of the blade. The rest of the surface was plain, if that can be said of highly polished steel, reflecting light like a mirror. Black and white leather covered the handle in a diamond pattern. The tsuba, or hand guard, was most beautifully carved with an eagle grasping a monkey in its talons on one side and an intricate floral pattern on the other.

She slid it back into the sheath. Still cradling it in both hands, she turned to Mushimo. He nodded and walked from sight. She followed reverently. The rest of the morning and most of the afternoon she spent resting in her room, surprised at the fatigue that had overcome her. She was fully recovered from her wound, so that could not be the problem.

The blade slid from the sheath so easily, and so often, that first afternoon. Over and over she studied the dragon engraving, her memory of the voices tempered with admiration. The sound had been so real, so disturbing. Several times she imagined that she could hear them again and slammed the blade home. She feared they might haunt her with the strength of their emotions. At first, they keened with brutality, fear, pain. With familiarity came honesty, strength of will, even kindness.

The flat of the blade felt so smooth under her fingertips. The touch brought a sense of calm, a self-confidence. For a moment she wondered if it was her own self-confidence or that of the blade.

Ridiculous! She shook her head and composed herself for meditation, the sword remaining within reach. As they ate that evening, it lay balanced across her knees.

"Mushimo, why did the voices stop when I came to this sword?"

Instantly, she wished that the question had been phrased differently. As it was, she suggested belief in their reality when what she wanted to know was if they *were* real.

"They were not the voices of the right one, the ones which spoke to you. When you approached that one, its soul enveloped you so that you could no longer hear the others."

"Its soul? You make it sound like it is alive."

She remembered the feeling of self-confidence.

"In a way it is. Its soul is the sum of all those who have owned and used it, even those it has killed. It found in you a kindred spirit, one which matched those from which it was made."

"But I don't understand its silence. Why would it not call to me and the others be silent?"

Mushimo grinned.

"I don't know. Perhaps like the men who used them, the weapons get tired of inactivity and their selfish natures make them try to lure you away from the correct one. Meantime, the correct one drew you in with silence, confident that you would find it in spite of the others." He shrugged.

"Are all swords chosen in this way? Did all the owners of this sword choose it as I did?"

"No. To both questions. Not everyone has the sensitivity you have. Some of my students have entered that room and heard nothing. And in turn, a few swords have no voice.

"This particular sword was handed down in one family for ten generations, perhaps more. Its entire history has not come to me. The line of that family has ended."

"Did you know the family?"

"Intimately. It is my own."

"Then I cannot accept the katana!"

He looked up sharply. "You refuse my gift?"

"No, but . . . Yes, I . . ."

"As I said"—his voice was hard—"the family line has ended with me. There is no one to whom I may hand it down. It chose you. I could not ask for more."

She stared into the darkness beyond him for several minutes, feeling torn about what to do. It didn't seem right to take what had been in his family so long. Yet, she wanted the sword. He wanted her to have it. She would accept it.

"I thank you for the gift."

She bowed. He smiled, satisfied.

She began practicing with the new weapon the next day. At first it seemed too heavy. She swung it awkwardly, often off balance. The spar came off best in their practice sessions more so than was usual. But she persevered. It was

her sword from the first moment she picked it up. It became
more and more hers each time she held it. There came the
day when she equaled the spar, fought it to a draw.

"Some day you will beat it," Mushimo said.

They walked together in the woods on a wondrously
clear spring morning. He seemed to lean on the staff more
than when she first came. There was silence between them,
the comfortable silence that exists only between true
friends. After a time, Mushimo spoke.

"You have been a good student, Laicy. One of my best. I
felt from the start that there was a bond between us."

"I remember the first test," she said. "I thought it was because Crowell was a link between us."

He nodded.

"It is time for you to go, I think."

She nodded. She had sensed they would part soon. She
felt also that something bothered him, something outside of
their friendship.

"Where will you go?" he asked.

"I'm not sure. There is something out there for me, some
magical purpose. I can feel it, almost a yearning for a thing
yet to be learned or experienced. A feeling like the one I
have always had about Musashi's book."

"I can feel it in you, like a call deep inside. I know in my
deepest knowing that you will find it."

They walked silently for a while longer, sadness already
gnawing at her.

"I'm not sure I want to find it," she said quietly. "I don't
want to leave here."

She looked out at the familiar, peaceful landscape, then
at the figure beside her. Was it possible it had been more
than two years since they had met beside the road? For the
first time she wondered how much longer he might live. It
was a sad thought. She shivered.

"I am comfortable here. I know my place, and I know

that I matter. Before, Crowell was the only one who made me feel that way."

"But it is time for your search to begin. There is still so much to find out about Laicy Campbell. When it is finished, you will matter even more."

"In what way?"

"In many ways. I am sure."

Arrangements were made within a week. Akiro was sad-eyed. The women servants cried. Mushimo said goodbye rather stiffly, then handed her a credit disc. He said it would take care of her needs until the search ended. She found out later how much it was worth. She had never thought of Mushimo as a wealthy man.

On the appointed day, she left the compound and walked alone to the road, where a car and driver waited. Her bags had been sent ahead and were already in the car. How it had been arranged she did not know for sure.

She decided to go home to Siebeling first to see her family one last time, but most of all to see Crowell. She wanted to thank him for the past two years, which had been his idea in the first place.

When he saw her, Crowell hugged her tightly and said he had heard from Mushimo how well she had done. Her mother and brothers were uncomfortable in a way that confirmed how much she had changed. In spite of that, she stayed four months—long enough for word to reach them that Mushimo had died.

3

The Quest

Laicy and Crowell sat at the table in his kitchen. Tears streamed from her eyes and rushed silently down her cheeks. She wanted to strike the stony look from Crowell's face, make him cry as she was. But it was grief that made her want to lash out, to hurt someone or something in retaliation. He reached across the table and squeezed her hand, hard. A single tear slowly spilled from his eye to trace the smile line around his mouth and drop from his chin. She placed her other hand over his, then broke free, jerking to her feet.

"I need to practice," she said huskily. "Will you practice with me?"

He nodded and followed her into the dojo. They began the ritual of donning the traditional clothing and armor. When she practiced alone with the spar, she never bothered with all of it. According to the old books, the attire of kendo had changed little over the centuries except for the materials out of which the articles were made: plastiwood substituted for bamboo in the men, or helmet, and the chest protector, or the do; artificial fibers in the cloth of the kote, or gloves; and the same fabric in the soft covering of the men and do. Other aspects of the art had changed or may have changed in varying degrees. But the basic ritual, the attire, and the weapons themselves were always of the old tradition. It was important at this moment to follow tradition.

They faced one another, bowed, then drew three steps closer. Shinai were drawn and crossed at the tips; then the opponents crouched on their heels. Swords still touching, they stood, right foot in front of the left, slightly apart. There was a long pause as they stared into each other's eyes through the bars of the masks of the men. Neither would ever be able to say whose concentration wavered or who swung first, but they fought furiously.

Several points were scored because of impassioned recklessness; there would be bruises for a time afterward, most on places not protected by the armor. Sweat streamed down their faces in spite of the absorbent hachimaki tied around their heads under the masks.

Laicy had the advantage of more recent practice with experienced adversaries. She was besting her erstwhile teacher when he suddenly took a one-handed swing, surprising her. His shinai struck her on the side of the men just above the ear where the heavy padding ended. Stunned, she crumpled to the floor. Crowell was beside her instantly.

"Laicy, are you all right?"

He struggled to remove the kote from his hands, then gently he unlaced her men and pulled it off her head. She moaned groggily as he cradled her head in his lap.

"Just let me lie here a moment," she said, tears easing out from under tightly closed lids.

He struggled with the laces of his own mask, trying not to move too much. He untied her hachimaki and combed her wet hair with his fingers, then removed the gloves from her hands. Her eyes opened, and she looked up at him for a long moment. She reached up with one hand and pulled his head down so that his lips met hers, softly. Kiss followed kiss, each more passionate than the last.

They fumbled with the bindings on their do and closures on the layers of clothing until at last they lay naked on the exercise mat. Their lovemaking was gentle and passionate, tentative and familiar, all at once.

Afterward, she lay there contentedly drowsy, her sweaty skin sticking to the mat. She rose when Crowell's shower cut off to take her turn. A little while later she entered the kitchen wearing one of his robes. Crowell stood at the stove fixing some tea, a gift she had brought from Earth.

She sat at the table watching him move around the small room. He avoided looking at her, concentrating totally on what he was doing.

"Crowell, what's wrong?"

He stopped moving, placed his palms flat on the counter, and braced himself. He stood that way for some time before answering.

"What happened in there shouldn't have happened."

His voice was full of remorse.

"Why not, for god's sake?"

"You were a virgin."

"So?"

"For Christ's sake, Laicy, I'm almost twice your age. You were my student."

It was then she realized that her education was not complete. She could not quite understand his reasoning. Of course, there were certain types of sexual behavior that were still frowned upon, but she was no child, and quickly pointed that out to him. She was, after all, nineteen years old, and most women gave up their virginity long before reaching that age: a fact of life, off and on, for many centuries.

"Not only am I a grown woman," she continued, "but it was I who chose to lose my virginity. You neither forced me nor seduced me. It was more the other way around, as I remember. I needed to feel the closeness and love of someone I care about. I'm glad you were there, and I love you for that."

She got her clothes, dressed, and left the building, left him standing in the kitchen, his back still turned to her. Before now, she had not realized how old-fashioned his thinking was. He would understand and agree with her eventually, she was sure, but for a time he would need to think it over by himself.

The next few days she spent at her mother's, clearing up the little things that still needed attention. Laicy transferred a sum from Mushimo's disc to her mother's account, enough to make working unnecessary for the rest of her life, then made arrangements for mother and the brothers to move to a better house after she were gone, and disposed of some personal items. The older woman thanked her, but with little enthusiasm, as if it were only to be expected. Laicy had the feeling her mother was dead, had died from the inside out many years ago, and wondered if her father's leaving was the only cause.

The old hatred for him did not rouse. Instead she was discovering a new curiosity. Her mother would not talk about him and was evasive when asked if there were any pictures. Once, while her mother was gone, Laicy looked through all the cabinets and drawers. In the back corner of a kitchen drawer she found what she wanted, wrapped in a tattered piece of cloth. It was an old-fashioned holographic cube. Laicy activated it. He was a rather handsome man. On the back was the name Jonathan Campbell.

Carefully, she rewrapped the cloth and tucked the cube into one of her own bags. He was, after all, her father, and there was always a chance, slim though it was, that she might see him in her future travels.

On the last day she sat alone in the living room, staring at the walls, trying to conjure up memories. The smell of the place, of age and damp and being worn out, made her nose crinkle. She had spent seventeen years of her life in this house. There should be something worth taking away. The one regret was that there were no regrets about leaving, probably never to return.

Everything was done. She could bear the place no longer, and walked out with her bags and didn't look back. All farewells had been said long ago. Except to Crowell. If he had gotten over his self-reproach, she would stay with him until the liner left. Otherwise, she would spend the two days at the hotel.

She spotted him in the street some distance from his house. *He's certainly in a hurry,* she thought. He waved as he spotted her and quickened his pace. As they drew closer, she could see conflicting emotions playing across his face and wondered what could possibly have such an effect on this usually composed man.

He came to her side and turned to walk beside her toward the house, waving a communication disc in front of him.

"It's from Mushimo's lawyers," he said tightly. "He left me everything. They confirm that he had no heirs."

"I'm not surprised. He was obviously fond of you."

"But, Laicy. This will change everything for me. I'll have to go back to Earth. I'm wealthy."

He was silent for several strides.

"I would have preferred that he had lived. I'm not sure what to do with this." He waved the disc again.

"First, you must go see his lawyers and find out exactly what his properties consist of . . ."

"There was one other thing," Crowell interrupted. "If what he gave you should be depleted, additional funds are to be put at your disposal."

"Depleted?" She gave a short laugh. "I had in mind to return some of it. That is, unless I am still wandering the galaxy when I'm old and grey."

They neared the entrance to his house. The dojo wing of the building wrapped around the side, making the street a dead end. Behind and to the side of that were sparse woods. It was quiet here, the crowds of people and vehicles left behind.

Laicy set one bag on the concrete, casually opening the other. Crowell's eyebrow rose in curiosity, joined by the other in acknowledgment as he continued to talk. Her hand reached inside the bag as he drew slightly aside, apparently still deep in conversation. In unison, they drew swords, she from the bag, he from his belt. Her katana glinted in the sunlight, while he held a shinai. They stood watching five black-clothed figures bear down on them from the corner of the dojo.

"Do you want my companion sword?" she whispered as steel blades waved.

"No, I think it's too late."

The ninja encircled them, and Crowell and Laicy moved until they were back to back. The five attacked all at once, managing in a short time to force the two apart. Her concern for Crowell, meeting steel with bamboo, receded as for the second time she fought for her life. Her sword met two, then three blades one after the other. From behind came the sound of a solid impact and a grunt of pain. Without looking, Laicy knew Crowell had scored. Her adversaries reduced to two as one ninja replaced his fallen companion.

A red haze spread over the scene, and to Laicy's amazement the ninja began moving in slow motion. The cuts and swings of their swords were equally slow, giving her more than adequate time to defend, find an opening, and strike. Visually her own movements were equally slow, but in reaction she was several times faster than her adversaries.

Dodging, parrying, moving in a circular pattern, she and Crowell managed to get close again, protecting each other's back. One ninja lay lifeless on the concrete, apparently from a blow on the head from Crowell's shinai. One of her opponents, moving so slowly, left an opening as the second backed away. The katana arced around, cutting the first in the right side. The blade went deep, and blood oozed as he floated to the ground. The man gave a cry of pain, distorted, drawn out. In the red haze it sounded more like a dull roar.

The second enemy lunged at her, mouth wide open, emitting a more shrill roar having no meaning. Quickly she sidestepped and swung her sword, catching him in the stomach with the point moving upward. His own momentum forced the blade deeper. She jerked the blade free from the quivering body, then wheeled around to guard against attack from the rear and to check on Crowell. She was just in time to see the final two ninja running back into the forest, their pace so slow she felt she could catch them in a moment.

She could hear herself panting for breath, inhaling so slowly that there seemed no way to get enough air. The red haze began to fade, and she looked at Crowell, whose breath also came in gasps.

"You okay?" he asked.

The sound of his voice was not yet quite normal.

"I think so." She looked down at her hand. "Just a little scratch." She held it up for him to see. The red haze was completely gone.

"How about you?"

"Cut on my upper arm." He flexed his right arm. "Doesn't hurt much." His voice was completely normal.

"Let's go in and I'll take a look at it."

She gathered up her bags, glancing at the bodies sprawled in the street.

"Guess we'd better call the constable too."

However, as soon as they entered the house, she dashed for the bathroom, where she gave in to the sickness rising in her stomach. Weakly she moved to the couch.

"I called the constable," Crowell said. "He'll be here in a few minutes." He looked at her closely. "Are you all right now?"

"Yes."

She turned and stretched out. How had that happened? During the fight she had felt exhilaration, excitement, from the contest, from fear, and from doing what she did well. The red haze had muted the excitement because of its strangeness. It wasn't until the realization struck her square in the stomach that she and Crowell were alive, unharmed, and that three people lay in the street dead that she began to feel sick.

Nothing like this had happened after the first time at Mushimo's. But then, her own wound had driven all other concerns from her mind. As she recovered, the first fight took on the aspect of a bad dream. This incident was very real, and she would never forget the slightest detail.

Constable Jackson arrived with two subordinates. His attitude bordered on rude, as if the whole thing was their fault. The town had little crime, he said, and he took obvious personal satisfaction in that. Having his record marred in such a bloody, violent way made him very unhappy. That the two kendoka could offer no explanation for the attack did not improve his mood. They did tell him about Crowell's inheritance, but that anyone could have found out about that so soon seemed impossible.

Laicy remembered Jackson as a quiet, unassuming man, or as unassuming as someone six-foot-nine could be. That memory helped to curb her temper a bit.

Once he was gone, she and Crowell discussed the little information they had.

"They were probably sent by the same ones who attacked Mushimo," she said. "He said there was an old grudge of some kind."

"Yeah, he mentioned the fight when he notified me you were leaving Earth. They must have been sent to keep me from claiming his estate. Or to complete their vengeance in some way."

"Do you have any idea who this old enemy might be?"

"None. It was in the background the whole time I was his student. Just little hints now and then. But he never spoke of it directly. I had come to the opinion that it had died."

He paused thoughtfully.

"They could have been after you, you know," he offered.

"Somehow I don't think so. Partly because they would not have waited so long."

She patted his hand.

"I am concerned now about your returning to Earth with the possibility of an unknown enemy there, waiting for you."

"If they're determined to get me, I doubt they would let my staying here stop them."

"All the same, you must be extra careful. Earth is their ground."

"You could come with me. That way we could protect each other."

"The thought crossed my mind, but . . ."

"But you've got this quest, or whatever," he finished. "I have a little more time to try to persuade you, though."

She looked puzzled.

"Remember? Jackson said we can't leave until he completes his investigation. Lord knows how long that might take."

Laicy smiled. From the look in his eye and his behavior, he had gotten over his earlier guilt feelings. She didn't question it, looking forward to the rest of her stay.

For several days she wanted to tell him about the experience with the red haze but hesitated, fearing there was something not quite normal about it. One morning, as they lay in bed, she told him. He laughed softly and pulled her closer.

"That happens to everyone who is a true kendoka," he said. "I remember well the first time it happened to me."

"The first time?"

"Yeah. If you practice enough, with superior adversaries, it might happen often. Not only in practice, of course. When the fight means life or death, it can happen with more rapidity. Regularity too.

"Some experts think that it is the prelude to achieving the void, that if you don't experience the red haze, you will never reach the void."

She snuggled closer, feeling much better about what happened, satisfied to be one step closer to that goal.

It took two weeks and three days for Jackson to give them permission to leave. The constable was unable to learn anything about the three dead, two men and one woman. No origins, nothing. The two who escaped simply disappeared like shadows at noon.

Staying together, living together that extra time, made leaving much more difficult for both of them. They decided, once Jackson gave them the nod, to make the break as quickly as possible. One of Crowell's students would take over the school. He found passage to Earth on Wednesday. She booked passage for the day after that. He didn't ask for where. Laicy knew he wanted to ask, to know some way of keeping in touch.

Laicy walked with him to the terminal. They sat waiting for the call for his shuttle, which would take him up to the liner. They held hands while self-consciously avoiding looking at each other. The call flashed on the boarding screen, and reluctantly they stood.

"Are you sure you won't change your mind?"

He turned to face her. His eyes glistened with tears. She shook her head.

"I can't. But I'll know where you are."

"Yeah."

He pulled her close and kissed her. She watched through tears as he walked away.

The next day she returned to the terminal to catch her own shuttle.

That was nearly six years and twelve planets ago, give or take a planet or two, each one chosen from the atlas for no apparent reason. The only connecting thread was that each was farther from the starting point than the one before.

More than once she thought of reversing her course and

joining Crowell. But something deep within kept her moving away.

She came to hate practicing alone. In her frustration she began provoking fights with others who thought they were good at hand-to-hand fighting of one form or another. None were good enough to beat her, but more than one had given her a good fight. She had a few more scars to prove it.

Such encounters were building a reputation and affording her greater experience as a warrior. In spite of that, she became less and less proud of such challenges as, occasionally, the reputation would precede her.

Only once did she come face to face with another ronin like herself, a classically trained warrior. They knew of each other's reputation before they met. Lucas Kent was an expert at karate and knew a little about kendo. For six months they trained together, teaching each other the art they knew best. They did not fall in love but were drawn together out of a kind of loneliness into making love, sharing everything for a short interlude. It was from him that she got the name Iroshi.

He called her that as a pet name, saying it meant "woman warrior" in some obscure language, native to some equally obscure planet. She liked it, the meaning and the sound, like a Japanese name, and decided to take it as her own. She thought of it as a shield between her old life and the one she was moving toward. It also reminded her, by its sound, of her two years as Mushimo's student.

The interlude ended as it began, in a natural, agreeable manner, each feeling the need to move on, in different directions. She learned bits and pieces about a lot of planets, met a lot of people. Most of them were content, living lives of productive security and, to her mind, boredom. True, they were colonists, living primitively compared with older colonies. But most were second-generation at least and cared little for adventure even while wrestling with cumbersome bureaucracies.

It was on Kelsey that she encountered the old man. He sat at a table in the restaurant when she walked in one day. She greeted several acquaintances, but her attention could not be drawn from the stranger. As she passed his table he looked up and nodded, then returned to his meal. She sat at her accustomed table and the waitress took her order.

"He looks like one you should take on," Tasko said, taking a seat across from her. He was a former navigator whose company she enjoyed.

"Who?"

"The old man. You noticed him when you came in."

"Don't mess with him," she warned.

"Why? Is your sixth sense telling you something?"

"Yes. He is probably the best warrior any of us has ever seen."

"How can you know that?"

Just as I know you want to challenge him, she thought.

"I can feel it," she said at last. "I will avoid any conflict with him at all costs."

"If you say so," Tasko said and shrugged.

He had seen her fight several times, she knew, and must know there was no glaring fear in her. The feeling was real and true, and she did not want to see Tasko get hurt. She liked him in a distracted way, the way she liked everyone these days, not wanting to form any new attachments.

Gradually, as she moved from place to place, she learned to control her frustrations and to learn from practicing alone all that could be learned. The reputation she was earning was a two-edged sword, sometimes tempting a fighter into a challenge, but just as often making him hesitate.

She was most comfortable with members of the navigators' guild. They particularly fascinated her with the way they linked with liners' computers, becoming as much a

part of the ship as was humanly possible. She listened over
and over to their descriptions of what it felt like and determined that some day, somehow, she would try it, even
though it required surgical implants in the skull and was illegal for someone not a member of the guild. She made
many friends in the organization, and if there was a way
she could find it.

The nearness of the ruins brought her back to the present.
The sand buggy bounced to a stop. A cloud of dust wafted
away from the vehicle as she climbed out to take her first
close-up look at her new home.

4

The Temple

The gate had come down long ago. So long ago that not a trace of it remained. Stones from the walls lay strewn across much of the entrance, leaving just enough room to get the sand buggy through on a meandering course, or so it looked. After noting that, Iroshi turned the sand buggy right, following the wall.

Yellow-grey stone, cut into blocks of varying sizes, had been used in its construction. Old stuccolike sheathing still covered a few stones. In some places, the wall was three feet thick, but nowhere was the wall complete enough to determine its full, original height. The tallest section still standing was about ten feet. Here and there, tumbled stones forced her to swing wide.

The gaping testimony of a second but smaller gate gave access almost directly opposite the first. Being narrower, the fallen rubble closed it off completely.

Back at the starting point, the odometer showed over a mile and a half around. She sat in the buggy just outside the entrance waiting for . . . an invitation? Was one moment better than another to enter unknown territory?

Iroshi climbed out, studied the buildings and lanes just inside. Straight ahead the walls of two buildings flanked an alley. It dead-ended against the wall of another building. Details merged in the shadows now that the sun had nearly sunk behind the western part of the complex.

She took a deep breath and eased the vehicle over the littered path. She crossed the threshold and stopped again. The shadows were cool after the heat of the sun. She shivered, not from the sudden coolness, but from a sudden thought.

What if she got into the complex and could not find the way out? It was a very big place. Probably a large number of buildings and streets.

"Stop it," she ordered out loud. Her form of claustrophobia: fear of being trapped.

Reason it out: to find the way out all she had to do was keep to the outer wall. She could follow it to either gate, or simply walk over the many spots where it had been breached.

There, she thought. *Move inside and get the first part over.*

She guided the buggy in. Within two turns she realized the streets were much too narrow. Just to the left of the gate she had seen a building that proved complete enough to hide the vehicle. She resumed the exploration on foot. Staying close to the wall should make it relatively easy to come back to the same spot.

She wandered among the ruined buildings. A kind of calm began to seep into her being. She was meant to be here, a kind of homecoming. This she knew instinctively; analysis would come later. First, she would let the feelings saturate her being. It was part of what had drawn her to this place. So much to understand, but knowledge would come gradually. This was not a time for active objectivity.

Twilight settled in as she completed the tour. It was time to set up for the night. Near the building where the buggy was hidden she found one of more substance than most: it had a hint of a roof. A couple of pegs and three shelves mounted in the walls sufficed for storing a few things. The rest could be unloaded tomorrow once she decided on a permanent place.

She lit the lantern and began to practice. Her own shadow became the adversary. The two shinai were evenly matched. She wore tunic and tights, as always enjoying the freedom of movement without the armor. As karate followed kendo, she became even freer, stripping to her underwear. The sword was her greatest strength, but there was a pleasure in feeling the power of her body, in knowing that it too was a weapon when necessary, which had been the case more than once.

She moved well. Lucas said that had she started with karate instead of kendo, she would have been very good. A kendoka also learned the art of kicks and hand strikes, but the sword was the main concentration.

Becoming one with your sword, achieving the state of mind, no-mind, was the aim of every serious kendo practitioner. There were moments when she thought this state of emptiness, the void, was within her grasp, when her movements were natural, without thought or fear. But they were moments only, fleeting glimpses of perfection, which slipped away unfulfilled. Satisfaction came in knowing that those moments occurred a little more often.

The void, or at least the struggle to achieve that state, was a mark of the ronin. So were the swords an unbadged warrior carried. Warriors who worked as bodyguards or in the entourage of corporate or world leaders always wore the livery and badge of their employers.

She sat down on the sleeping bag, wiping the sweat off her face with a towel. It was a good way to stop the train of thought. Such employment had at first seemed the ideal way of gaining more combat experience. The memory of those conflicts was almost as bitter as that of the fights she encouraged as a ronin.

Next she would be remembering Mushimo and Crowell, missing them, wondering if they would be proud of or disappointed in what she'd become.

These memories were a product of practicing alone. She finished toweling off and slipped into the sleeping bag. It had grown steadily cooler since sunset, as happens in most deserts, but heat still emanated from the stones of the walls. The desert air smelled clean, even in the ruins.

Overhead, bright and dim stars blinked at her. She lay

watching them, thinking of the future rather than the past. Tomorrow she would begin the job of looking for water. There had been water when the temple was built, she was sure, but the source could have been destroyed or simply dried up in the intervening centuries. In isolated religious establishments, the source was usually hidden. Especially if the culture had been prone to wars of any kind, or so study of history had told her. But that had been Earth's history, and the same on two or three other planets she had stayed on long enough to read a few books.

The size and construction of this complex led her to believe the society had been both religious and warlike. Taken altogether, that meant water would be very difficult to find. She yawned and drifted into sleep.

The greyish-white sky was just getting light when she woke. She missed the blue sky of Earth so much, even though it was as far away in time as it was in space.

Hastily, she pushed such thoughts aside, trying to concentrate on the dream. In it she had found the well, still filled with clear, fresh water. An overpowering fear swept through her again. There was danger, but it had not been clear.

Iroshi closed her eyes, rebuilding the feelings, letting memory flow backward and forward. The outline of the building grew clearer, but the memory didn't help that much. A dozen or more of the same appearance must be scattered about the complex, which might consist of perhaps fifty to seventy-five buildings in all.

She shivered as she dressed in the cool air. Breakfast consisted of a wafer with a swallow of water. Then the day's search began. She marveled at how the roof on nearly every building was gone but the walls all stood, although in varying degrees of ruin. By midday she marveled at nothing, cursing instead her stupidity. Too many buildings looked alike, the passageways were a maze. It could take months to find the water.

A methodical search was impossible until she had a thorough knowledge of the layout of the buildings. But that would also take too long. Instinct had worked in other places for other reasons, but so far, in spite of the dream, she held back, not quite ready to give it free rein because of danger only sensed in the dream . . .

Instinct was the only thing she could rely on in this search. There was no one here with the knowledge she needed who could give it freely or have it taken from him. She began wandering aimlessly, allowing curiosity to guide her footsteps, the special sense to rouse the curiosity.

The building right there might be the one. She walked up the narrow stone steps, three of them, stepped across the threshold into the shade from the walls. The sudden coolness was a reminder of how hot it was out in the sun.

Slowly, she examined the inner walls of the first room. The small blocks, common in the buildings, were almost completely stripped of stucco covering. Most of it covered the floor as dust and small pieces. She kicked the debris around to examine the floor underneath.

Five rooms in the building. None of them had any particular significance. Disgusted, she stepped into the alley. The sun was lower in the sky, suggesting strongly that it was time to head back to camp. Carefully, she started in that direction, certain that she would at least recognize this building again. She made it with only three false turns.

Gloomily she ate and finished off the water in the canteen she had carried around all day. A whole day. Wasted. She tried to meditate before practice, but her spirit was in a turmoil and would not be calmed. She picked up the shinai and began. The feelings of frustration built into a rage as she lunged and cut with the bamboo sword. Iroshi took a one-handed cut viciously, throwing herself off balance, and fell face forward into the debris and sand.

She laughed softly. What a sight it must be, a kendo expert sprawled in the dust, covered with it, a victim of her own temper and her own shadow. At least it had improved her mood.

She completed practice with a calmer mind and, after cleaning up, crawled into the sleeping bag. That night, and the next two nights, the dream returned. Each time it was clearer, more detailed. The well was in a cellar or underground chamber of some kind. But when she searched by day, there were no buildings with access to below ground. And she searched very hard, using all senses, every daylight hour.

It was mid-morning of the fourth day. Iroshi wandered through the first chamber of a building, her sixth sense pulsing insistently. The room was larger than most, making it seem more important. She moved to the center of the room and looked up through the roofless space. This had been at least a two-story building, she realized. Then suddenly, with a loud crack, the floor gave way under her.

The fall was long, straight into utter blackness. With little thought she relaxed her body, ready to roll as soon as her feet touched. The big shock came when her feet touched water instead—cold water. She plunged deeply below the surface. Shock paralyzed her. Precious moments were lost. Never a strong swimmer, she broached the surface just in time.

Gasping for air and treading water clumsily were all she could manage for several minutes. The chamber was black except for muted light coming through the new hole overhead. Awkwardly, she searched her pockets for the small torch. They were empty. Panicking, she tried all her pockets again. Her head slipped under once, twice. The torch was gone, lost in the fall. Or perhaps she hadn't brought it.

There was no way to tell in which direction to swim. She was tiring rapidly, the cold water sapping her strength, and a slight cramp worked in her right calf. One way was probably as good as any other. She paddled straight ahead, until her fingers scraped painfully against rough stone. Her head went under again. She reached upward, desperately trying to grasp the rim. Not far enough. On the second attempt she kicked harder, springing higher out of the water. Her fingers gripped the rough edge in spite of the pain in her cheek where she had scraped against the wall.

The rim was high. It took all her remaining strength to pull herself out. She slumped on the edge, legs dangling, feet still in the water, gasping for air. In time she could breathe more easily. Time to examine the predicament.

There wasn't enough light to see a thing except an occasional shimmer on the surface of the rippling water. She called out. The sound disappeared in a big emptiness, too vast for echoes. There weren't a lot of options. Or maybe too many.

She stood unsteadily, shivering with the coolness of the dark, the wet clothes, and the more basic chill of fear. She needed to move, to warm herself, but which way was safe? Were there more pools of water? An exit, probably a staircase, must be somewhere. If it was still in usable condition.

She moved away from the water, hands outstretched and feet testing each step. It seemed like hours passed in this way before her hands brushed against another rough surface. A stone wall, feeling slightly damp, smelling strongly of the musty odor that pervaded the entire chamber. Keeping her left hand on the wall, she moved right, slowly. The sound of one foot following the other, tapping and sliding in the dust on the floor, filled the chamber and her ears. Every so often she stopped for a dose of silence and to allow her other senses to get their bearings.

All at once her hand slid off the wall into emptiness. She waved back and forth, encountering only more air. She leaned a now sweaty forehead against the coolness of the wall, feeling her heart beating in her chest, pulsing in her neck, hearing it roaring in her ears. Her breathing again was rapid and shallow. Sweat added to the dampness of her clothes. She shivered convulsively, knees buckling. She caught herself with a great effort. Training slipped away. She wanted nothing more than to scream. Instead she yelled as when lunging with the shinai, a kiai, long and loud, emptying her lungs. Then a long, slow-drawn breath.

She planted her left palm firmly against the edge of the wall and stretched, spread-eagled. Stretching, until her waving right hand brushed against another wall. The vacant space must be an opening into a second chamber. The exit might be through there. Searching more than one room, in utter darkness . . .

She could handle it. She could! If she had to.

With the same slow progress she continued. Out of nowhere a shaft of light shot across the chamber. After so much darkness it was blinding even though small, about the size of the beam from a small torch. As her vision cleared, she followed its direction.

A stairway! In the far corner. Quickly she maneuvered across the littered floor, afraid that the light would disappear too quickly. She clambered up the stairs, tripped, made it to the top to find—nothing. Two blank walls, one directly at the head of the stairs and one along which the stairs were built. She pushed against both. The light was beginning to fade. Beaten, she leaned against the side wall, sliding to her knees. The wall gave way, dropping her, sprawling, into a first-floor chamber.

After a moment to catch her breath, she pushed hurriedly to unsteady feet. Her hands shook as she picked up a piece of chipped stone to mark an X on the door. She made her way outside, carefully staying close to the walls, making several more X's ending on the wall outside. Working her way back to her building, she tried to memorize the route.

There was no warmth in the sun, although her wet clothes were beginning to dry. She shivered. Tomorrow she would find the hole that let in the sun's light and try to enlarge it. That would not only let in more light, but it could be used as a safer entrance to the chamber.

She didn't practice that evening, and bad dreams interrupted her sleep off and on all night, even though the lantern was on. Next morning she awoke too tired to carry out any plans for the day, and perhaps a little feverish from the dunking in the cold water and the chill of the black chamber. She spent the day reading and sleeping occasionally, a luxury she rarely allowed herself. Sleep was better that night, and the following day she felt more fit to start work.

She must relocate the chamber, and she began to doubt that was possible. Her memory was hazy. Nearly half a day of searching passed and she began to grow alarmed, wondering if it had all been a bad dream or if finding water in the first place had been a miracle not to be repeated.

It turned out to be neither; the building was right where it should be. The realization that she had passed it at least three times, from the wrong direction, was more than a little maddening. If she had only turned the corner . . . Instincts must have taken a vacation.

A careful examination of the outside wall did not reveal the opening through which the sun had shone. However, she discovered a hidden entrance when she leaned against a block elsewhere in the foundation, giving her another fright as it gave way. Perhaps her instincts were not so far off after all, she thought as she looked inside. Behind the block a second staircase carved from the native rock on which the building stood led down into the cavern. Her hands began shaking the moment she started down the stairs. Once at the bottom she could scarcely hold the lantern steady. Before she walked over to the pool she placed two small torches, one at the base of each staircase.

She did not linger at the staircase that had been her earlier exit, feeling a strong need to get out. But she could not leave until the fear was faced directly.

The light from the lantern reflected from the quiet surface of the water, nearly two feet below the edge on which she stood. The pool was roughly circular, the steep sides hewn from the rock. One edge butted against the outer wall. She judged it to be about twenty feet across. She took the canteen from her belt and dipped it into the coolness. Her hand shook, but not as much as before. The gurgle sounded very loud as ripples expanded. The water tasted pure and cool, just as it had in the dream.

For nearly a week all went as she wanted. In the mornings she continued the exploration of the ruins. They were vast; nearly seventy-five buildings was nearer the mark, each consisting of several rooms, with a few exceptions. The labyrinth writhing through the underground darkness she could not bring herself to explore, but she could guess that it was equally vast. The former tenants had left little else behind.

At noon each day she ate, usually a light lunch, then read for a time from her collection of book tapes, followed by a period of meditation. The amount of time for each activity was not set, only the order. She merely took as much time as seemed right.

Often she debated with herself over what was the most important part of the routine, particularly in relation to achieving the void. Would emphasizing meditation bring it closer? Was there a balance between meditation and practice that she had yet to find? Every day she pursued the void where "Everything becomes itself and nothing." Those were Mushimo's words. When he had practiced, and in the fight with the ninja, she had seen his oneness with the sword. His actions and reactions had been without conscious thought.

Crowell had achieved the void, but not to the same degree. Only in Mushimo had she seen total oblivion at any time he chose. She asked him several times how it was achieved but the answer was always, "You must find your own path."

She vacillated between despair and determination. The spark was there, and that kept her trying. At times she was sure that spark was growing, if only minutely.

After meditation, she practiced. The sun was usually low in the sky, the air beginning to cool. She made an effort to use each sword, as well as the other weapons stored in the bags.

On the night the change began, she was using the katana, the gift from Mushimo. Its balance was perfect, the handle almost exactly shaped to her hand. She loved using it, the way it sang as she spun it overhead, moving from one position to the next and the next. She could scarcely feel the weight as she defended against an imaginary enemy. With a yell, she went on the attack. Relentlessly, she forced him back. He was barely able to defend himself against the quickness of the assault. Clang of sword against sword filled the twilight. Victory was nearly hers . . .

The point of the sword struck the stone wall. The vibration of impact stung her hands. She halted in surprise, automatically checking the blade to make sure it was unscathed. In the waning light, it was difficult to tell.

She realized she was wringing wet when the cool evening breeze sent a rare gust over the wall. Shivering, she went for a towel to wipe away the dampness, puzzling over the unmistakable scent of cherry blossoms.

She sat on a stone block, wiping her face. What was happening? The opponent had seemed real, someone with a sword whom she nearly defeated before he disappeared. Was that the void? If so, it was not as she had imagined it. There had been no mention of encountering shadows there. Maybe it was a ghost out of the past, one that claimed the ruins as its own. Or, just as likely, a ghost from her own past.

There had been no sense of recognition. She found herself trying to recall his appearance, but could remember no details other than the action. The incident haunted her. *He* haunted her, her thoughts and dreams, with his faceless presence. From that night, she never again felt entirely alone.

5

Madness

Iroshi peered around the corner of the building, back in the direction from which she had come. The feeling of being watched was a constant prickling at the back of her neck. But there was never anyone there, anywhere in the ruins. She turned her back against the wall and slid down it to sit in the sand, head resting on knees. Either she was losing her mind, or the place was haunted as Constable Mitchell had said.

Two days had passed since her encounter with the shadowy swordsman. Two days of rising paranoia, and two nights of little sleep. Her head came up, determination on her face. It was time to leave, if not the planet, then at least the temple. As things were going, no goals could be achieved here. Finding the void, discovering the reason for the quest were more important than the fearful curiosity nagging at her mind. Curiosity about what had happened that night came over her each time she practiced. Who or what was the swordsman? She no longer believed that it had anything to do with the void. Maybe those mysteries would be solved in another lifetime. Or at least in another place.

She returned to the campsite as daylight faded, firm in the decision to start packing in the morning and to leave in the next few days. There were a few things to put back in the condition in which she had found them, including the water chamber. For some reason it was important that not just anyone stumble onto it. She grinned at the choice of words.

"Laicy."

The voice whispered. Her head snapped up. Muscles tensed. She sat perfectly still, hoping it would speak again to give a sense of direction. Her hand moved, slowly, toward the hilt of the sheathed sword lying close on the sleeping bag.

She listened intently for several minutes, but no further sound came out of the night except those that had become familiar. No voice called her name again, the name she had not used for years. Nothing breathed nearby. Or moved among the debris of her building.

Her sight turned inward, studying feelings, some old but not felt in a long time. Fear stood first among them. Fascination with what was or was not happening was a poor second, tied with frustration at not being able to figure it all out. Deeper, however, knowledge lurked not quite perceived, seeming to float, not quite anchored so that she could grasp it.

She shook her head, cursing under her breath. If it were possible to meditate, she could probe for that knowledge, but she had not been able to concentrate for many nights. That had badly affected her practice. If only Crowell were here, he might know what it was all about. Ghosts were not logical.

It would be wonderful to think the ghostly fight was part of the natural path to the void, but there was a wrongness with the idea. There was also a wrongness in thinking of the event as evil, although that was the way she perceived it.

She stretched and yawned. Too much tension and too little sleep were taking a toll. Although it was still early, she lay down on the sleeping bag. Maybe tonight sleep would come. Just before she dropped off, her hand again wrapped around the hilt of the long sword.

Tumbling into darkness, falling, falling without end. Hands clutched at nothing, trying to grasp something.

Mouth stretched wide in silent scream. Mind numbed with fear.

"Laicy, look out!"

She jerked awake, instinctively rolled over still clutching the sword. A laser rifle fired, striking the sleeping bag. The stench of burning insulation permeated the air. She pulled the sword from the scabbard just as the gun fired again. She raised the sword awkwardly, off balance, in a useless defensive move. The beam hit the blade, wrenching it from her hand. The energy of the beam scattered visibly in large and small sparks. The sound of muted voices rose into the night silence. It must have been the sound of the blade vibrating from the impact.

There was no time to think about it. She rolled again, this time into dark shadows in the direction of the sword's flight. Then she got up on hands and knees to scramble behind a pile of rubble once the weapon was firmly in her hand again.

The beam probed the darkness twice as she watched. She located the point of origin atop the outer wall of the next building. Her own guns were stashed in one of the bags laying in the light of the lantern. No way to get to them without being seen, shot, disposed of.

There was a moment to wonder who they were: the man who shouted the warning and the person who fired at her. Clearly two different people. It would seem that someone had decided to track her from Spencer. Maybe for the credit disc, although it was difficult to use one illegally. But why wait so long?

Her intended assassin could, of course, be a ninja. It had been some time since the encounter on Siebeling. But that didn't mean they had given up looking for her, *if* she had ever been the target.

A laser flashed, concentrating on the pile of stones behind which she crouched, scattering fumes. She turned away quickly, but fumes burned her throat and eyes. Tears filled both eyes, ran down her cheeks. Momentarily blinded, she shifted to her left slightly.

"Be still," the voice warned. "They hear you."

She froze. Where was the voice coming from? It seemed to be . . . No, that was impossible. No time now.

The tears washed her eyes clear as she stayed hunched down. She concentrated on the most immediate problem: a plan was needed.

"If there is a friend out there, he will just have to follow my lead," she thought.

Another probing beam. She screamed in terrible pain and dropped to the ground, lying on her back. Someone yelled, "Got her," then she heard thuds as two figures jumped from the wall.

Their cautious footsteps entered the room. One pair stopped; the other moved toward the hanging lantern. Both resumed their stealthy path toward the pile of rubble, angling together around the left side. Her boots came into view. They eased around, the larger man holding the lantern high.

She struck the instant they realized she wasn't in her boots. One horizontal cut and the big man dropped, his spinal column severed. The smaller one turned, crouched, pistol barrel coming up as she prepared to swing again. He screamed in great fear and dropped the gun. She completed the swing, the blade catching him on the right shoulder, cutting diagonally downward. He crumpled to the ground like a suddenly emptied bag.

She stood, breathing hard, holding the sword aloft, ready to strike again. There was neither sound nor movement from the two dark masses on the ground. She whirled around, remembering the voice. Someone else was there, somewhere.

Still fearfully alert, she moved around the bodies and picked up the lantern. For a moment she held it directly over them. No doubt, they were dead. She hung the lantern back in its place and moved the sleeping bag into a shadowy corner, nearly collapsing on it, as the trembling began.

Two more men dead. This time she had not sought the fight. Rather, she had shunned the people of this colony, tired of endless fighting as a ronin, the senseless violence in search of a reputation, finding someone better, someone worse.

Now, someone else was in the night. After the spectral fight, two days of paranoia, and no sleep for two nights.

She sat, eyes closed, leaning against the ancient wall, letting the trembling work its way through her body. Slowly she began to clear her mind, concentrating on an internal vision of a lighted candle, its flame sputtering as the air moved slightly. Unconsciously she swayed with it, the most basic of meditation.

The candle faded, replaced by vistas of a world passing beneath her. The worlds changed each time she meditated, but were always ones with which she was familiar. This world was unknown, an odd combination of lush forest and barren desert. Yet, there was a familiarity.

"Rune," she whispered, and knew in speaking the name that it was right.

With knowledge came a feeling of home. Joy spread through her being, as if she were seeing the world through someone else's eyes and emotions. That brought a touch of fear, and the vision was gone. Iroshi looked out from the dark corner, tears in her eyes, sorry that the vision was so short-lived. And curious, and afraid still, about where the vision had come from. It was not the Rune she knew.

At least the trembling had stopped.

She sighed. Such an unfortunate turn of events. The temple had seemed so right at first. But her desire to leave was even more vital, and tonight's deaths must be reported to the constable.

A pair of feet, sheathed in sandals, appeared as she stared at the ground. Very slowly she raised her head, letting her gaze climb up the full-cut brown trousers. As she reached belt level, the man's voice boomed out. The language was completely unfamiliar, but the tone decidedly angry. Chest-high and a shaking fist appeared, its whiteness contrasting sharply against the brown shirt. The face was contorted in anger, eyes staring straight at her. She felt nothing, as if emotion were suspended. No, it was more like she didn't accept his existence. The numbness did not last.

Fear exploded in her mind, blinding her for several heart-beats. She traced the passage of time by that beating. Nearly paralyzed, she was barely able to cringe against the wall as the apparition continued to subject her to his tirade. Yet he kept his distance, a fact she noted only marginally.

Just as suddenly as he had appeared, he was gone. Iroshi swallowed hard, glanced furtively around. It was still too dark to see anything distinctly.

Too dark? But he had been quite clear. Apparition, she had called him. Perhaps that was exactly what he was. Created in her own mind to torment her. But surely he would have spoken English.

She shook her head, as much as an outward confirmation of the frustration building up inside as an attempt to clear her mind. If she wasn't crazy, she was certainly on her way. It was time *now* to clear out of this place. She tried to stand up.

Nothing worked. Her legs would not unbend. Her arms hung uselessly by her sides, hands in her lap.

Voices drifted in on an early-morning breeze. They sang, a song so sweet and sad, and she didn't understand a word. They drew closer, entered the room. The beings looked very much like the first man in their costumes and ethnic features. Slowly they marched around and around ignoring her presence, intent only on their song. Eventually they exited as they had entered, their song fading away as though with distance.

Iroshi came to herself, having been nearly mesmerized. She tried her legs once more. Not a twitch. She called herself mad, screaming it into the dawn air. Either that or someone else was . . .

That thought could only have come out of madness. There was one way to be sure. Desperately she worked to compose herself for meditation again. Her mind struggled to regain control, as if it feared what madness made her suspect. It took hours to beat down conscious thought and to delve deeply into the other self. The one that sensed things before they happened. Felt the weariness of a machine through her hands. Knew the ultimate goal of the quest but had never revealed it.

Deeper and deeper she turned inward. Once she saw two of her selves merge into one. Most images flitted at the edge of seeing. She searched deeper, deeper than ever before. Until she saw him. Waiting. For her.

6

The Joining

She had found him. Now what? They looked at one another, she in total confusion, he in utter tranquillity.

He seems to think he belongs here, she thought. Aloud she said, "What do you want?" It seemed a logical beginning.

He opened his hands at his sides, palms outward, and raised them slightly. His silence was annoying, but she tried to emulate his peaceful attitude.

"Who are you?" A different tack. She hoped desperately for some kind of answer.

My name will mean nothing to you but it is Fons Ensi Fae Goron. I was called Ensi.

"Was called. I don't understand."

I am no more. Not in the way you think of existence. I can explain it all in the manner in which we are now communicating. It will take much time. Or, there is another way. . . . He paused, significantly.

"Something you will have to talk me into doing?"

Yes.

"But it will be much faster?"

Yes.

"And why will I probably not want to do it?"

Because it is frightening to relinquish control of one's mind, one's memories. Especially to a stranger, an alien, whom they cannot see. It is even more difficult for someone like you, who never gives up control to anyone. Ever.

Her heart rate jumped, nearly calling her back to herself. He was right, but how did he know?

"I can't think of any reason I would want to do that, or anything you could say to convince me to trust you that much."

Even her thoughts trembled.

Mushimo.

"Mushimo? What about him?"

We knew him.

"We?"

I knew him. In the same way I am asking you to try.

She sensed truth in his words.

"Mushimo died," she said, feeling the sorrow intensely even after the years that had passed.

I know.

"How?"

We felt it when it happened. And I saw it in your mind. I was not prying, he added. *The feeling of loss is so sharp and fresh within you that I could not avoid it as I passed.*

She would try what he asked, she decided abruptly. There was probably no other way to extricate herself. If Mushimo had done the same . . . Well, he survived intact.

"All right. What do you want me to do?"

She could almost hear a sigh of relief. *Just relax. Let me guide you, show you my world.*

She breathed deeply, gradually easing further the tautness of body and mind. The panorama of a world passed beneath her, the same world she had seen the last time. Rune, with the odd mixture of desert and forest. The view flickered several times as she tensed and relaxed in turn. The scenes had a quieting effect, and the flickering reduced to almost nothing.

This was my world as it looked when my people and I still walked its surface. We called it Nevas.

There were many large cities with all the problems inherent in such places: crime, poverty, graft. Some people lived more isolated lives in farming communities—a few by choice, but most by accident of birth. Others tried to completely isolate themselves in the mountains and deserts.

Iroshi saw glimpses of each feature as he named it. Just enough to grasp the essence.

I was a member of a uniquely isolated group in this temple.

It came into view. From above, it was as much a maze as from the ground.

We were priests and priestesses, religious men and women, worshipping violence as much as we did our gods. Here, we worshipped Sooneen, Nolav, and their son, Yelda. In all the temples and sanctuaries, we trained and lived as much as warriors as priests. But there were too many different sects throughout the land, too many warrior leaders who would be Tahreen, or supreme leader. We were constantly at war, supporting one or another claimant to numerous thrones.

The temple bustles with activity. Men and women practice martial arts, some are at their prayers, and still others supervise and help in the everyday operations of such a community. From appearances, they come from several ethnic backgrounds, attested by different skin tones, facial features, and profusion or lack of hair. Everyone wears the same rather shapeless pants and tunics, negating prior social status. The colors vary, signifying the rank or stage of training that the wearer has attained in present life.

A messenger approaches Ensi in the practice yard where he directs the exercises of several acolytes. The message comes from someone on the council summoning him to a meeting. As combat ward, Ensi is automatically a member of the ruling council. He turns over the class to a lieutenant and rushes away. It is an unusual time for a meeting.

He enters the council chamber, his soft shoes allowing him to cross the stone floor silently. He pauses before the crescent-shaped table, bows to the councilors already there, and moves to his seat. Yon, glaive ward, Garon, truth ward, and Savron, body ward, return the bow; then the four wait patiently for Aicir, spirit ward, who as the eldest, both in age and precedence, presides over the meetings. His position as chief priest has no bearing in this selection.

Soon, Aicir enters. He bows in his turn to the other members and takes his seat. He called the meeting, and it is obvious the cause troubles him deeply. No one else speaks. Aicir remains quiet for several minutes. The others wait politely, quietly, but anxiously.

Word has come often in the past few months of rampaging armies of the Tahreen to the east. He has often voiced his desire to occupy this temple, knowing of its supply of water and, further, coveting its position on the frontier of the badlands.

Aicir's reluctance leads the others to fear the worst. Usually he is blunt, outspoken, although not unkindly.

He raises his head and looks intently at each of the wards in turn, as if to impress every feature on his memory. As he looks them full in the face, the expression of sadness in his features is even clearer. Finally he speaks.

"The army of the Tahreen approaches. It will be here tomorrow afternoon."

This is the turn of events they have all dreaded. It explains his reluctance. This is the largest of the armies, and the deadliest. Their very numbers will nullify the superior skills of the small force occupying the temple. Each councilor knows there is no reprieve. The close proximity of such a large force, approaching from the east, makes escape impossible. And the Tahreen will show no mercy.

To the west waits the greatest desert of the land, the badlands. The temple was built just within its boundaries, right over the last source of water. Crossing that wasteland is a test of courage very few can pass.

The templers are trapped by their own history and traditions, and just a little by their pride. Running away is not to their taste, and running straight into the steel of death is no less so.

"The younger acolytes will be sent over the wastes to the mountains," Aicir continues. "They are young enough to have the best chance, few enough in numbers to move rapidly, yet numerous enough to carry a large amount of water. As well as some of the manuscripts.

"A token force will meet the army here to give them a chance to make good their escape. But a token force. No more."

They look at one another, wondering at his last words. They know him well enough to know that there is a plan of some sort. The pause stretches out, leading them to believe that he contemplates something fearful.

"You have heard of 'revay'?"

The members nod, surprise now reflecting strongly on their faces.

"You know then that it has been only a theory, a legend from our past, never documented as tried successfully."

They nod again.

"I have managed it successfully. Five times. I know that is not enough to make me an expert, but since we will all die anyway . . ." He shrugs. "We've nothing to lose."

"Would it not be better to die fighting?"

Ensi speaks softly. As chief warrior he cannot help viewing this as the more honorable course, and a better example for his students.

"No," Aicir answers. "We have come too far, learned too much. We cannot let it be lost. I intend to take as many as possible. Once it is done we should be able to learn even more in our new state of being. Some day, we will know how to pass the accumulated knowledge on to others."

"But to live without a body. To have only intellect and emotion."

Savron shakes her head. She is a doctor, body ward. Without physical bodies, of what use are her skills?

The discussion begins, continues until after darkness has fallen. Ensi argues long that he should stay and lead the warriors who are to be left behind. Yon argues, like Savron, that without bodies his skills with making and maintaining weapons are useless. Garon says little. As truth ward he deals primarily with facts, the intellect, but he is as torn as the others. The truth he sees in Aicir's suggestion and arguments render him speechless until at last he must argue on the old man's side. There lies the truth.

In the end they decide that volunteers will fight the holding action. The arguments are resolved one by one. Most importantly, all five wards will go into revay with a large number of the priest-warriors.

The order is given for the horns to sound, and templers—priest-warriors, truth-sayers, neophytes, and workers—assemble. The wards look out at them from the balcony, shared sorrow striking with full force. Aicir explains what is happening, the decisions that have been made. Volunteers are requested, and more than needed step forward. The young neophytes, twenty-three of them, separate from the rest and are quickly outfitted for their dangerous trek. A few argue to stay but are soon convinced that they must try to survive to nurture and carry forward the beliefs and knowledge accumulated by generations within the walls of the complex. They carry with them some of the most precious writings of their predecessors as they file through the west gate, their exit cloaked by darkness.

All who will go into revay assemble wood for pyres, except Ensi, who works with the volunteers on their final battle arrangements. One small group of warriors will wait to light the pyres when the time comes, before joining the battle at the outer wall.

One at a time Aicir guides his people to a stack of wood, where they lie down and listen to his instructions. It is a long task, and he wonders if it can possibly be finished, much less totally successfully, before the army arrives. He feels so old. Ensi enters, and Aicir motions for him to take the next place.

"I will be last," he says.

There are tears in his eyes for those he has just left at the walls and from the still strong feeling that he should be with them. Aicir nods and moves on.

Next is a young woman, Andray, whom Ensi has often
noticed. She is pretty, more so than ever as she composes
herself on the stack of tree limbs and wooden planks, her
eyes closed and her breathing even as she listens to Aicir's
instructions. Either the old man is getting better with practice or she learns more easily than many of the others, for
her breathing ceases very quickly. The spirit ward moves
on to the next, and Ensi touches Andray's brow tenderly.
The body will soon be beyond the look and feel of death.
Now it is still warm and soft, and he regrets not approaching her before.

The sun has lifted above the horizon as Ensi at last lies
down on a pyre, relaxing as Aicir speaks to him. All the
years of meditation, inward looking, help him to concentrate on the words. The sounds of the approaching army
reach his ears. His spirit rebels, and Aicir coaxes his attention back. Soon, his breathing too stops.

Aicir rises, stretching his old body. He nods to the group
hovering nervously around the fire in the center of the
arena. Quickly they dip torches into the flames and begin
their unpleasant task. Aicir takes his place and closes his
eyes. For a moment his thoughts linger on the others, a
tinge of fear for them in this new journey makes him
shiver. The torch bearers finish their work quickly, not
wanting to linger, wanting only to join the battle alongside
their comrades.

The sounds of battle rise, then subside. Fires rage, black
smoke billowing into the morning sky. The templers fight
well, managing to hold back the enemy until after midday.
None are left alive when the Tahreen leads his army
through the alleys and streets of the temple complex.

The Tahreen is furious when he finds the mounds of hot
coals and ashes in the arena.

"How dare they kill themselves! That was to have been
my pleasure. The cowards."

He raves for an hour or more, striking those of his ret-
inue nearest him like a spoiled child throwing a tantrum.

He orders the temple razed and all its treasures brought to him, then turns his mount. He will camp several miles away. The stench of death does not agree with him. He disappears into the shadows beyond the arena.

He cannot know that he is watched. Nor do his men know it as they begin the work as ordered. Swords and other treasures are gathered. Items of precious metals and jewels, gathered by the templers over many generations from generous patrons, they carry away. Paid soldiers value only these things, ignoring the few books left behind and the tapestries and paintings. These are simply piled up and burned as part of the destruction of the complex.

But a few of its former inhabitants are already learning. Voices whisper in the darkness; a few small articles move of their own volition. Not very much, but enough to scare the wits out of soldiers, always superstitious men. They leave hastily, their task only partly completed, hoping as they run through the night with their booty that the Tahreen will never have any reason for or means of knowing later.

Ensi and the others rejoice in the small victory, even while they grieve over the damage that time will enlarge upon. There are other reasons for grief.

Aicir takes a count as soon as the army leaves. Three of their number have not made the transition, leaving them at sixty-three. Not bad for a first-time effort. One of those who is not among them is Andray.

They made real discoveries in the first few minutes of their new lives, and the following weeks were full of many more. That they could communicate with one another had been taken for granted and, happily, was the case. A few found they could communicate with people outside the complex, although the communication was usually confined to receiving information and only rarely involved giving it.

For some time, this was their only contact with the rest of the world, the means by which they observed the steady rise of civilization and its eventual demise. Nevas became a desolate unpopulated world. It took many lifetimes for its natives to complete the work.

The reasons for the death of civilization and its practitioners were many and varied. Disease and war, and the diseases brought by war, were among them. Natural disasters added to the problems. A worldwide drought, turning more and more land into desert, was the final blow. The planet was just beginning to recover by the time Iroshi arrived.

The passage of time waxed and waned for Ensi and his companions. Through the centuries, the millennia, those in revay learned more and more about themselves. Their individual powers grew, and they learned to work collectively to accomplish more difficult tasks. One of these was to establish any sort of communication over great distances. They could not leave the temple but if they stretched themselves, sometimes forming a chain by combining their energies, they could "be" anywhere on the planet, or on another one, but the effort exhausted them.

They also learned to enter the bodies of those who happened into the compound, but never how to do it without the host knowing something was happening, even if subconsciously, and being driven away in fear. Their presence became subtle but never completely unnoticed.

They communed with one another, learning what each one of them knew, thinking at times as one mind. They grabbed bits of information and knowledge from the occasional unwary traveler. From their accumulated knowledge a plan, a purpose, grew. Something for the future. It was given added impetus when they met Mushimo, a remarkable man. He was the first, and until Iroshi the only, one able to accept the presence of one of them. Only he had been able to talk with them, give them information about conditions of the known worlds and his own kind, and accept their plan.

"Miss. Miss. Iroshi!"

7

The Plan

Someone was shaking her, calling to her. It was a struggle to open her eyes, but Iroshi finally managed it. Everything was dark, including the figure crouched over her, still shaking her, calling her name.

She moaned, and he lifted a lantern to see her face more clearly, illuminating his own at the same time. It was Constable Mitchell from Spencer. He helped her sit up.

"I thought for a minute you were as dead as those two." He motioned with his head. "Looks like they've been dead for a while."

He paused, waiting for her to say something. Iroshi just sat where he had placed her, supported by his arm, face expressionless. With his free hand he lifted her chin so she had to look at him.

"Are you all right?" Her eyes focused on his face.

"Yes. I think so. Been ill." She sounded as confused as she felt.

"What happened to those two?"

"Killed them."

"I guessed that," he said gently. "Why? Did they jump you or something?"

"Yes. In the middle of the night." Her voice was slightly stronger.

"That's their style. They probably figured out someone was here and came in to get whatever was worth taking. Surprised they came in here. Most of the prospectors avoid this place."

"How did you find me, then?" Her mind was getting back in operating condition.

"I drove out this way, which I do every so often, and saw a dune buggy partially hidden behind some rocks close by. Remembering our conversation, I thought it might be yours and decided to check. I found their footprints, knew they weren't yours. I followed them here. Your lantern was still burning." He looked around the room. "You must have been quite a surprise to them."

"It was mutual." She sat up straight, away from his supporting arm.

"Care to give me the details?"

She did, dispassionately and briefly. Up to the moment she sat down against the wall. Throughout the telling, her mind blocked out what occurred afterward.

"And what happened to you? I mean as near as I can tell, that all took place about two days ago. Give or take an hour," he added, looking up at the lighter grey sky overhead.

"Two days?" It wasn't possible. It was just last night. Wasn't it? "Are you sure?"

"Like I said, that's as near as I can figure it. You don't appear to be wounded. Said you were sick?"

The last words were spoken almost as an offering. She felt sure that he was looking for an explanation that would keep her out of trouble with the law. But why? She had after all failed to report two killings, an oversight that even in a place like this could be a serious offense. She nodded.

"Yes. I had been sick for a couple of days before they came. That and the shock of what happened must have been too much."

How easily the lie came. But not a total lie. How many days had she gone without much sleep? She certainly had not been at her best.

"Well, you can come back with me so the doc can take a good look at you. I'll have to start . . ."

"Oh, no," she interrupted, thinking of Ensi. "I mean, I

can't leave my things here, and I am feeling much better. I should be, after two days of sleep."

She smiled and held his gaze a long moment. The guilt of the lie made her break away first.

Without a word, he moved to the task of gathering up the bodies. Shaken, she joined him. Together they carried them to his sand buggy and struggled to get them into the vehicle. He took hold of her shoulders when they had finished, turned her to face him.

"The magistrate isn't going to like my not bringing you in. I'll be back in two days to make sure you're all right and let you know how everything goes."

She nodded. He placed his hand under her chin, forcing her to look up again.

"I'll be back."

"But I am fine."

"I'm not sure of that, and I don't think you are either. There's a touch of madness in your eyes that wasn't there before." She tried to turn away. "Two days."

He released her and climbed into the buggy. The wind blew exhaust fumes directly at her, making her cough. She stood perfectly still as he drove away without looking back. He grew smaller with distance, the dust trail thinning as he turned onto the hard-packed road.

For a while she busied herself shoveling bloodstained sand into a bucket, then carrying it out to dump it in a nearby isolated alley. Once it was all removed she smoothed the remaining sand over the spot. Just that little activity, following the trip to the buggy, drained her, and she sat down against the wall. "Ensi, are you there?"

I am here, Laicy.

"Has it really been two days since . . ." She groped for a single word to describe their meeting.

Yes, it has.

"And you were telling me . . . uh, showing me Nevas and your people the whole time?"

No. As soon as we sensed the constable's approach I re-

leased you. You slept for about three hours before he ar-
rived.

"That means I've only had three hours sleep in, what,
nearly three days?"

About that.

"I still could be hallucinating. Perhaps losing my mind."

You do not believe that.

"No. But I almost wish I did. I am too tired right now."

She lay down on the sleeping bag.

"Wake me in a while and we'll continue."

Ensi didn't answer, for she was falling asleep.

Iroshi walked briskly past the water building, turned the
corner and headed back toward the camp. She was beginning to feel much better after nine hours sleep, a little food,
and a long walk to stretch tight muscles. So far, Ensi had
remained silent and she had not called him, but he was
there. She could feel his presence, if only slightly. She returned to the camp, feeling more relaxed. Making herself
comfortable, she called him.

"I am ready," she told him.

Very well. I have told you about me and my people,
enough to start with anyway. Is there anything you would
like clarified so far?

There were so many things. What to ask first?

"I want to know about Mushimo and the plan you spoke
of. It sounds so mysterious."

Not really. You understand, of course, that all we had to
do for a number of centuries was think about such things.
Discuss them. Until we refined the ideas to our satisfaction.
We considered all the frailties inherent in a civilized peo-
ple. But first let me show you our encounter with Mushimo.

He is young but clearly Mushimo. His carriage and air of
confidence confirm a youthful resemblance to an older, .
well-remembered man. He enters her building, where his

own camp is set up in the same room. It has a settled look about it, as if he has been there quite some time.

His attitude is one of listening, but he is alone. He is communicating with one of the Nevans; their conversation becomes clear.

"But, Aicir, if she comes with me, she may never come back." Mushimo's thoughts are first.

"We know that, Mushimo. She knows that. But in order to search for the one to carry out the plan, one of us must accompany you." Aicir pauses for a moment. Mushimo waits for him to continue. "Just as we were sure for some time that you were the one, so might you be confused. There must be more than one to watch and listen.

"With the training you will give your students, and sending them out into the inhabited worlds to teach, the search will be dispersed. More students will be found, sent to you and Fotey to teach and screen. Each student who is not the one will be sent out as a teacher, until their numbers grow. They will be the basis for the Guild of the Glaive when the time comes.

"But it will take two of you to do the screening. One opinion would not make a clear decision. It will also keep too many people from learning about the temple."

Mushimo nods. "I understand all of that. But what will such a separation do to her? She may be gone forever."

"We can never be completely separated. Our thoughts move between us no matter the distance."

"How can you be so sure? None of you has ever traveled far."

"We know."

"And when I die?"

The thought is soft, as if the mind can be muted just as the voice can be.

"With luck, someone will have proved worthy of receiving Fotey. Perhaps one of your sons."

Iroshi was jarred from the scene. Sons? Mushimo said

there were no relatives, no heirs. What happened to those sons?

Ensi would not answer, saying only that she would know later.

Too many questions were piling up, unanswered. She wondered if it would ever be possible to get them all satisfied. Wondered even more why she believed, trusted, this voice from inside her own being.

She turned away from Ensi and refused to acknowledge his presence. This whole thing was becoming too much of a strain on her nerves and credibility. Control was in his hands, had been from the beginning. She had given it to him at one point, she couldn't recall when, and now she wanted it back.

When she was younger, both Crowell and Mushimo had chosen the moment of revelation. But at twenty-five and after six years of complete autonomy, being treated like a student again made her angry.

When she was ready to reestablish communication it was to be on her terms, beginning with her name: she was not Laicy. For her, the name had been left behind along with the girl to whom it belonged.

"When I began this quest," she explained later, "I felt that I was starting an entirely new life. Some of it has not been cause for pride. Except for Crowell, there is no need for anyone else to ever know of me again. I am not even sure I would want Crowell to know of some of the things that I . . . that happened."

It was all part of the learning and growing process, Ensi explained gently. *How can you know truth without recognizing lies? How can honesty be clear to you without seeing its opposite? How can you know love without feeling hate? In order to truly teach something, one must first have the experience.*

As for your name. We call you Laicy for one important reason. Since no one else calls you by that name, these days, you will always know it is one of us.

"You mean there are others who can get inside my mind?"

There are many beings from different worlds who are capable of thought transference. Including some of your own species.

"My species? You know of intelligent beings other than humans?"

Of course. At least we knew of them at one time. Several visited this world long before you humans did. We overhear whole civilizations from long distances. Some of them have disappeared, and we heard their death struggles. Others are too distant for us to know what became of them.

One thing you must understand, Laicy. We Nevans were not humans. We were humanoid.

"You were not human?"

She had assumed, from the visions . . . Ensi's presence took on a more alien taste. There had been no visible differences.

"Was everything you showed me true?"

The possibility of hidden lies was occurring to her—lies in the reasons for contacting her, in the nobility of his people, shadowy possibilities clear only to alien minds.

Laicy, you can trust them as I learned to.

Mushimo? That was his voice. But how? He was dead.

Ensi will explain in time, Mushimo's voice said inside her head. *I speak to you now only to reassure you, to keep your doubts from preventing your accepting and learning. You will have the truth about me, about everything, soon enough.*

In the meantime, learn from Ensi and the others as you once learned from me and Crowell.

"Mushimo."

He lives. But . . . Of course, like the Nevans.

"All right, Ensi, I am ready."

• • •

What we call the plan, for want of a better term, is to save your species from self-destruction, a path on which it seems deliberately bent.

"That seems a large undertaking."

Perhaps. But we saw our own species, and several others, virtually destroy themselves, and we recognize the signs. Some of the others were near extinction when we first encountered them. However, yours is the most extreme case. If we can give to humankind our accumulated knowledge, maybe we can save them, with their mostly unwitting help. We have learned that it takes time to achieve nobility, but there must also be strength.

"But didn't Mushimo explain to you the condition of humankind? We have spread throughout the galaxy, too far and too fast. No one, nothing, controls this so-called empire. Worlds and groups upon worlds work at cross purposes.

"The only semblance of control comes from big corporations, especially the mining companies. The larger, more powerful families rule their own worlds. On others it's the guilds. Each group is protective of its sphere of interest, looking out for its own welfare. The hell with anyone else."

Yes, Mushimo told us of that. Nothing has changed since he was here. We have picked up information from others. But it is not impossible to save man from himself.

"But why do you even care about what happens to humanity?"

Having nothing at risk in life's events gives one the option of embracing everything. We can neither love nor hate, not as we once did. We can feel happy and sad; can identify injustice; can care, but not about individuals or a single world.

Iroshi sensed the difficulty Ensi had choosing the right words to describe the existence of souls, intellects, the entire essence of being, entities that had no bodies. Whose world had ceased to exist centuries earlier. Beings who could feel the existence of others but who could interact only with those who came close enough.

We have reached the point in our existence when we must contribute. We can no longer just watch and learn. Our knowledge is in a state of completion where we can do much good.

Ensi continued explaining. It was a complicated plan that would take years to bring to fruition and that would begin with her "discovery" and translation of old texts within the temple complex. Based on the knowledge within those texts, Iroshi would establish a guild of warriors and truthsayers. They had thought of this organization as the Guild of the Glaive.

Its members would be hired by business leaders, industrialists, and world leaders as bodyguards and witnesses. It was projected that they, or their talents, would become valued as the best of their kind obtainable. They would bring innate abilities, honed within the Glaive, magnified by an unseen companion, one of the spirits of Nevas. Their services would be very expensive.

While Glaive members would make themselves indispensable to civilization at large, no permanent assignments would be accepted. Moving each member from one assignment to another would help ensure complete neutrality, of the individual as well as the entire Glaive. When they proved themselves proficient and beyond reproach, the Glaive would act as a unifying force, ideally, with enough influence to intervene in conflicts, sway opinions, and steer decisions. But they must always work behind the scenes.

Finding the right candidates for membership would be a difficult beginning task. The screening process must be perfected to the point of infallibility, if such a thing were possible. True, they could not be gods, even though they had the ability to look into minds.

At this point Iroshi broke in.

"I can understand that all of this should prove quite lucrative for the Glaive, enough to maintain such an organization once it is established. But what are we going to start with? I mean, just going through channels for licensing as a guild takes a lot of credits—for bribes, fees, paperwork. Even the credit disc Mushimo gave me could not begin to cover it."

We will provide the funds. You see, along with the ancient texts, which in themselves will be worth a fortune, you will find an enormous treasure.

"A treasure? Where?"

Within the temple. The Tahreen and his men missed the greater part of it.

"How did your priests come by such riches?"

We were always receiving donations from rich noblemen and ladies. Some of it was donated to the temple, some was given to us for protection. A portion was won in combat of one description or another, over many centuries. That was the treasure the Tahreen sought.

"Where is it?"

We will show you later. When we guide you through the whole of the complex. There is much you have not yet seen.

"Always later! You ask me to trust you implicitly. But you cannot trust me in return."

Ensi stuttered the beginnings of a reply, then fell silent. Was it a desire for caution or just a shortage of time? What she had been told so far could never be proved, nor could it harm or betray the spirits in any way. However, it galled more than a little that they would hold back even though they had obviously been aware of her for a very long time. They knew her faults, strengths, weaknesses, and abilities, or they would not now be trying to enlist her in this cause. They fully expected her to accept what they said, to become a participant, to eventually lead the effort, while they continued to treat her like a novice, a student, or as someone not yet trusted.

Then too, impatience was one of her greatest faults. Mushimo tried to teach her that she could not learn everything at once. Perhaps she had jumped too soon.

We do trust you, Laicy, Ensi said suddenly. *We intend to be totally honest with you. But we are very new at this, just like you. We have thought it all out, and the principles are sound, yet we must proceed slowly for a time until we are sure beyond a doubt that we are succeeding.*

To us you are a student, you are very young. Your own experiences, past, present and future, will become part of the overall pattern, like a woven cloth. Your spirit will permeate every facet of the Glaive. So much to do and learn. It will be exhausting. It is important that the plan be initiated correctly and smoothly. There can be no faltering later.

Iroshi assured him she wanted to understand and asked him to continue. He did with clear relief.

Once disposed of, the treasure would finance the founding of the Glaive, the search for the first initiates, and the rebuilding of the temple complex for its headquarters. As the search progressed, and during the entire building process, Iroshi would study the ancient texts and everything that the spirits could teach her.

All those who entered the Glaive were to have extensive training in the arts of combat; many from Mushimo's own school would be sought out. However, there would be several members, the most honest, who would concentrate their skills as truth-sayers.

A truth-sayer, Ensi explained, *is one who will answer a direct question with a direct answer, without guile. Such a person says only what he or she knows to be true; no guessing or repeating rumors. In dealing with a truth-sayer, the art is in asking the right question. The value of such people will be as witnesses to agreements and contracts, and their honesty must be established beyond reproach.*

As leader, Iroshi must master this discipline too, but she would be exempt from the oath of truth-saying. A leader always has secrets.

Eventually, Iroshi would hire agents to search for special weapons, such as her own sword. Some, already trained as warriors, would bring their own weapons. But each would have a "weapon with a soul," which she could provide from the collection. Such a collection of arms would be a source for young initiates who would someday get their full training within the Glaive.

The size of the membership would be limited to sixty-two, the number of Nevans available for bonding with a human host. Such a limitation would make the Glaive itself more manageable, its secrets well kept, while making them a very rare commodity.

"It all sounds well planned," she commented. "But I am not clear on what you hope to accomplish. You have given me only generalities, no specifics, about how we are to save my race. Of what benefit will our efforts be to the worlds of man?"

There is a great deal we hope to accomplish, but some plans will be made as we go along. As for what we worked out during our years of near isolation, well, it is long and detailed. It might take years to explain it all. Your kind is approaching the point where self-annihilation could become inevitable and irreversible. And the possibilities are still numerous.

"Our end has been predicted before."

But we have seen the signs in others.

"Are you saying that humankind may soon disappear?"

Not as a species. Not yet. As you pointed out, its society, civilization, has reached beyond its capabilities. By expanding its civilization outward so fast and so far, it has stretched too thin to control the edges of its empire, and in trying to exercise control, it weakens itself even more. It has exceeded its capacity for communication, and that capacity is vital to continued existence.

A unifying force, a common base, must be created, brought into play. That will be our strength. We can communicate across great distances with the speed of a thought. Can you imagine what effect that could have in a society accustomed to waiting weeks, even months, for a message?

"Instant communication. From one end of the empire to another?"

Exactly. With the knowledge we gain from ability, and the trust we will build for the Glaive, the trust of all the powerful men and women, in all areas . . .

"Control! Is that what you are seeking?"

No, Laicy! Not control. Influence. Guidance. Persuasion. Achievement of a common purpose. Coordinated action.

"But, I . . ."

You think you are not strong enough. The thought of leading such an effort frightens you.

She shook her head. He must have sensed the movement, for he continued.

That is where we must start, now. With you. Already, there is much raw knowledge within you; some Mushimo awakened but did not hone, leaving it for us to do. Some has not yet even awakened. Earlier, did you not block me from your thoughts? You were never taught to do that. There are many such things you know how to do, instinctively. All we need do is make you remember them.

"I have never even managed the void. How can I . . . You are asking me to go beyond that point." She felt totally inadequate.

You are closer to the void than you think.

That night she dreamed of Mushimo, Crowell, Ensi and herself. They tried to convince her to do something, all talking at once, as she practiced with her sword. She couldn't make out a word of what they said. Suddenly Constable Mitchell walked in, ignoring the other men. He took her hand and without a word led her from the room.

8

It Begins

Iroshi opened her eyes. Blinking away sleep, she was not surprised to see Constable Mitchell sitting on a large stone some way off, watching her. She smiled at the memory of the dream.

"Well, I'm glad you're happy to see me," he said.

She laughed. If he only knew how happy she had been in the dream.

"It's been two days," he said by way of explanation.

She crawled out of the sleeping bag, brushing at her clothes. She picked up the bag, shook off the sand, then folded it away.

"You look better than when I last saw you."

"I feel better. Did the magistrate give you a hard time? About my not being there."

"Yeah."

From the tone and the look on his face, it was an unpleasant memory.

"Sorry. I never meant to cause you trouble."

He shrugged, the gesture like that of a young boy who has been caught in the middle of mischief and doesn't want anyone to know he cares. She offered him a breakfast bar, which he accepted along with some water. He took a deep drink from the canteen, then contemplated it very seriously before handing it back.

"Iroshi, do you have any idea how long you've been camping out here?"

She swallowed the water, then capped the canteen. "Not very long. But exactly how long? No."

"Two months and a few days."

"No! Not that long."

She was genuinely surprised that it had been so long. Why the matter was of such interest to him she could not quite guess.

"Where do you get the water?"

He looked at nothing on the far wall.

"I brought it with me," she said warily.

"Not that much." He was so intense.

"Ensi," she thought. "Can you read him?"

A moment.

She kept her eyes toward the ground at her feet.

He does not appear to be suspicious of anything in particular. I think he is confused about why you are here. Especially a woman of your reputation.

"Nothing else behind his questions?" she asked, wondering what exactly was meant by "reputation."

Nothing except his training as a police officer.

"Can we trust him?"

He is an honest man.

She considered that answer. Honesty can be either a blessing or a curse, used for or against. So far, Mitchell had shown a kind interest in her welfare.

To Mitchell she said, "I found water here."

He looked up, eyes wide in disbelief.

"I'll show you."

She decided on impulse, the germ of an idea beginning to grow. Was it her idea or something planted by Ensi? Did it really matter if they were one?

She stood, held out her hand to help him up. His grip was pleasantly strong. Once at the subterranean pool, his disbelief scarcely abated.

"Never dreamed there could be so much water in a place like this," he said as Iroshi lit the second torch, by the other stairway. Two torches and the lantern Mitchell held over the pool brightened the chamber considerably.

He stretched out on his stomach and reached his arm

down to set the surface of the pool in motion with his fingers. She said nothing, reading his reaction: amazement, of course, but something else directed at her.

"How'd you find it?"

She pointed to the ceiling. The hole was still there, a light grey in the blackness overhead.

"You didn't."

She nodded, grinning. For the first time she could see a touch of humor in her tumble through the floor, enough to match the good fortune she had already recognized. Having someone else to share the memory chased away some of the tendrils of fear that crept in every time she entered the chamber.

"I assume there was no light in here then."

She shook her head.

"How did you find your way out?"

"Very awkwardly."

She pointed to the staircase tucked into the far corner.

"A shaft of sunlight lit the stairs. Once I could see the way, I got out fast."

He walked around the edge of the pool, then along the four walls.

"Have you done much exploring?" He thumbed at the black maw opening into the next chamber. A momentary chill raced through her at the memory of her hand plunging into that vacantness the first time. He didn't notice, still contemplating its hidden depths.

"Not yet," she answered. "I plan to do some detailed exploration down here later. I am still getting familiar with up there." She pointed at the ceiling. "It is like a maze. Ready?"

She waved toward the exit. He nodded and started out as she cut off the torches. Once outside in the sunlight, she carefully concealed the opening.

"A real surprise," he murmured. "Why are you so secretive about it?"

"Can you imagine how many of your prospectors would

flock here if they knew there was water? I want peace and quiet."

"But no one ever comes in here."

"Two did just recently," she reminded him. They walked along slowly.

"Were you looking for water or just wandering around?"

"I was looking for it. I suspected there was a secret source of water, or at least evidence that there had been one in the past. If you study the histories of temples and religious societies, they were often built over or near a spring or well. Especially those in the middle of nowhere like this one must have been. In many cultures, such large complexes, both the occupants and the site, became involved in wars and lesser conflicts. The very size of this one indicates it has been here, well used, for many centuries.

"There are always exceptions, of course. But so far everything I have learned applies to this temple. Of course, we will never know its entire history."

"Sounds like you've studied these things."

"I have. You sound surprised."

"I am, a little."

"Why?"

"Well, you know." He turned, embarrassed, which she found thoroughly charming. "A warrior with your reputation wouldn't seem to be the scholarly type."

"What reputation?" She touched his arm, turned to face him. "You said something like that before. I know I am not unknown on many of the colony worlds. But exactly what have you heard?"

"That you were in the habit of picking fights." He looked her in the eye, as was his habit, daring her to deny it.

"Is that all? Those old stories preceded me? Yeah, they usually do, although I have not heard them all. Actually, not many of them, but enough to know how I am usually pictured."

She waved her hand in the air. "It is not a period of my life of which I am particularly proud."

"Why did you do it?" His voice was matter-of-fact. She couldn't tell if he was just curious or was judging her.

"Many reasons. And excuses. I guess I was trying to prove something to myself and everyone else."

"What?"

She shrugged. "That I could do it. I wanted to reach the void so much. Practicing—even with someone—just wasn't enough."

"The void?"

"Yes. Oh, you don't know kendo or Zen, do you?"

"Uh-uh."

They were back in her building. She made up a pallet on the ground for them to sit on.

"A student of kendo, at least the way I was taught, must some day learn to enter the void before becoming a master. The void is a state where the warrior becomes one with the sword, with the person she is fighting, with her surroundings. Other weapons are used in other disciplines but a kendoka uses the sword."

She got the bag containing the weapons and sat back down. From the bag she took out the steel sword, the katana, wrapped in a soft cloth, unwrapped it and pulled the blade from its sheath. Its sheen mesmerized her, reminded her of the day she received it, as it always did. She set the sheath aside, cradling the sword, hilt on one palm, blade on the other. Bowing from the waist, she handed the weapon to the constable.

He took it just as she offered it, replacing her hands with his, without taking his eyes off her face. Once he felt the full weight, he looked down. No one had held it but she for a long time, and a sudden fear that he might not give it back washed through her. He handed it back.

"Show me."

She bowed as she took it, rose to her feet, bowed again. She went through several basic moves—thrust, cut, stance—in rapid succession, yelling out the name of each invisible target: *men, kote, do.* Her front foot slapped the ground as it led her forward. The blade flashed in the sunlight, moving so fast it seemed to sing as it sliced the air. He was, in turn, mesmerized.

She stood still, bowed once more, and sat down. Ritually, she wiped the blade, replaced it in the sheath, and wrapped it in the cloth. Her vision was turned inward, and he probably wondered if she was aware of his presence. Once the sword was put away, he spoke.

"Impressive."

"Thank you." She focused on him.

"Don't you need someone to practice with sometime? Fighting the air doesn't seem like good training."

"It is best with a partner, of course. There was plenty of practice when I spent my time in schools. The teachers were both expert, and I learned more because of their undivided attention. Now I must use the spar."

"I've heard of them but haven't ever seen one."

"I will show you."

Out of another bag she brought the spar, a round object, about four inches in diameter.

"The two spikes are transmitters and receivers. They detect the position of the swordsman and transmit a beam according to that information and the settings."

"How do you turn it on?"

"Here." Iroshi handed him the spar, which he held gingerly, as if it might explode any minute. She pulled a small control box from the same bag.

"This"—she pointed at an old-fashioned pressure pad on the control box—"turns the spar on and off. This one"—her finger moved to another—"sets the height. The dial determines the level of expertise. The lowest setting is strictly for the novice to practice swinging the sword against an object. The next few settings are for practicing offensive actions.

"Defense is more difficult. The settings for that are the next higher group. The highest ones include both offense and defense.

"This is an older model. Some of the newer ones have many more settings, and are all voice-activated. I prefer this type because it is like the ones I used sometimes in school."

"Can hitting a beam of laser light feel like another sword?"

"Yes. The biggest difference is in the sound. Blade against beam simply cannot sound like blade against blade, whether steel or bamboo."

"Can you show me how it works?"

Iroshi hesitated. It had been a long time since she had practiced in front of someone. Not since she and Lucas . . .

"Sure, why not?"

She moved away, strapped the control to her left wrist, and drew the shinai out of the sword bag. Hand poised over the controls, she turned back toward him.

"Don't get any closer to me or the spar. The beam is six feet long. It is not strong enough to kill, but it can give quite a jolt."

He nodded.

She touched the switch and a faint hum came from the spar. The second switch made the ball rise from the sand until it was shoulder high.

The machine attacked first, sending a blue-white beam of light from one of the spikes. Iroshi blocked, blade buzzing against beam. Machine and warrior jockeyed for position. Iroshi sensed Mitchell's surprise, then admiration, and was irritated at the girlish pride she felt. His presence was distracting. She concentrated on the power of her voice as she yelled her aggression.

A beam nearly tagged her as she reached to the controls to cut it off. She grinned as the spar settled back onto the sand. Wiping away a little sweat, she began putting everything away.

"Is there any way you can beat that thing?"

"With this." She pointed to the control, then unstrapped it and put it in the bag, her grin mischievous.

"Funny," he said as he grinned back.

"The only way to win in the upper settings is to break the current of air it rides on."

"Where did the name come from?"

"Spar?" Everything was put away, and she sat down beside him. "I don't know. I tried to find out when I was on Earth but never did. I figured that the name must be very old."

"You've been to Earth?"

She nodded. "Many years ago. I studied there for two years."

"Kendo?"

"Yes. Plus history and philosophy."

Listing the others was not a lie, although she had studied neither formally. She had read a great deal during those two years on both subjects, an interest that she still maintained. If she was to find and translate the texts of which Ensi had spoken, establishing herself as a knowledgeable student was important.

"Is that why you've traveled so much?"

He was very casual, she thought, remembering their earlier conversation.

"To continue my studies? Yes. Each colony has yielded a separate chapter in the history of our race. A few worlds had histories of earlier, indigenous civilizations, like here. Each one became the source of lessons, about myself and my abilities."

"And a reputation."

"Apparently." She laughed, then said seriously, "As I said before, some things I did are not cause for pride. But they all gave me valuable experience. I got better and better."

"But not good enough to reach this 'void'?"

"No. Not yet. Sometimes it seems so close. You see, in kendo, to win is to die."

Mitchell's eyebrows came up.

"Not literally. But when one achieves the void she becomes, not just herself, but the sword, the opponent, everything. The self is lost; it dies. It is all things and nothing . . ."

"Hold it!" He held his hand up. "Sorry, but there's no way I can understand such things. I'm no deep thinker and, to be honest, I've no desire to be one."

"Okay. I won't try to initiate you. It's just that my quest for the void and my love of history are what led me here. Especially to this temple. I *feel* something about this place, call it my sixth sense if you will, and I became so engrossed. I guess that's why I did not realize how long I have been here.

"But back to this reputation I am supposed to have." She grinned at him again. "What exactly have you heard?"

He began reciting some of the tales, each more fantastic than the one before. She laughed at some of the adventures she had never had, on worlds she had never seen. She found herself telling him the truth about those with some basis in fact. Like the fight on Talus against a man also wielding a sword.

The story went that she had killed the man with a magical sword that had appeared in her hand from out of nowhere. The truth was that sword and scabbard were concealed under the long cloak she wore, and the sword was drawn by her own hand. Luckily, it was the first occasion she had achieved the fast draw so many ronin work for. It saved her life on that occasion, for the attacker had no intention of giving her any opportunity to defend herself.

Other stories unfolded, and the realization came to Iroshi that such a reputation, no matter how unearned, could prove invaluable if the Guild of the Glaive began to form. It remained to ensure that the legend not only survived but grew.

"That is amazing," she said with a laugh, as he ran out of stories. "Not only that these stories are told and retold, but that you remember so many. Funny, people believing them, true or not, but some things that really happened they probably would not believe."

"Like what?" He was all attention, a believer in the legend of Iroshi and one who would spread it.

"Right here, for instance, when those two thugs attacked me. The first time one of them fired, I was off balance. I had the katana in my hand. Without thinking I raised the blade and the beam hit it, bounced off into the night. The sword was not only unharmed, but it sang with the impact as if it had a voice."

The awe in her own voice was not feigned as she recalled the sound of the metal vibrating. But from a greater distance in time, she wondered.

Mitchell reacted just as she would have predicted: with amazement. She was also sure that the incident would become part of the legend.

They talked until early morning, when he rose to leave. Iroshi suggested that he get some sleep before returning to Spencer, but he insisted on going. His way of looking at her every so often made it obvious that he would like to do more than stay and sleep; he was also in awe of her and could not yet presume. She, on the other hand, felt things were complicated enough without pursuing a romantic relationship, and she did not insist that he stay.

They said their farewells. He promised to return soon and sped off in the sand buggy, disappearing immediately into the darkness beyond the light of the lantern, as the engine's roar was flung behind. The headlamps lit his path, then they too disappeared.

Iroshi returned to her room and began practicing in earnest. Beams slashed outward in rapid succession. The sword glinted in the lantern light as she anticipated each attack, then launched her own. Sweat dampened her clothing in the cool morning air.

The world glowed red. At first she thought it was a trick of the sunrise. As the speed of the beams slowed, she recognized the time-dilation phenomenon. The beams took forever to move, so that she had more than enough time to counter.

The shadow warrior stepped from behind the spar. It was impossible that the tiny orb had concealed him. The spar settled to the ground out of the way. The two swords met, joined, one as real as the other. For Iroshi, the red haze and slow motion persisted.

Sparks from the striking blades kept time with the sound of their meeting. Back and forth the two figures moved, cutting, then passing through. Every move had a counter-move. Every step a counterstep.

The katana became an extension of her arms. She felt the friction as it sliced the air, a faint hum spreading from sword tip to toes. Meet the blade. Defend. Attack. Keep moving. Forever. She flowed like the wind, feeling but not touching. Knowledge of every move coursed through her mind as she plucked the strings. She knew.

A myriad of life energies coalesced into one, not her, not them. Different and the same. The swords cut and met. They sang. Her voice joined theirs. Lathra, Rune's sun, added the sounds of the newly born morning. The world was one sound, one movement, all in harmony. They could go on forever.

Iroshi stood with the sword held upright at arm's length, breathing hard. Feeling nothing, and everything. She came back to herself, out of the void, as a single person. She smiled.

Congratulations.

"You knew?"

Yes. I too was a part of you, and you part of me. It will become easier now if you do not let it go.

"Never!" Her breathing slowed. "Did you send the war-rior to me?"

Yes.

"Who was he?"

The old man you would not meet, from before.

"In the saloon."

Yes.

"And I beat him?"

You did.

She sat down slowly, unable yet to release the katana.

"It was wonderful."

And Constable Mitchell? You will not let him go?

"I have plans for him. In the Guild."

As a warrior? The thought didn't please Ensi.

"No. More of a manager. Our liaison with the outside world."

She smiled again.

"I think he is too practical to believe in ghosts."

PART II

9

Guild of the Glaive

Iroshi stood on the platform applauding with the visiting dignitaries as Constable Zack Mitchell became governor of Rune-Nevas. Mitchell raised his arms overhead, accepting the congratulations. Only Iroshi saw the discomfort in his eyes as he turned to look at her, then turned to the others on the platform, completing the turn to face the small audience again.

Everyone resumed their seats as the applause faded. Iroshi scanned the faces below. A few more than a hundred were permanent residents, nearly the whole population, sitting with warriors and truth-sayers of the Glaive recalled from their assignments to attend the ceremony. The Glaive was the basis for what economy existed on the planet, except for the few prospectors still combing the wilderness seeking their fortunes.

The population was sparse in spite of the growing fame of the Glaive, and Iroshi was determined to keep it that way. Having Mitchell named governor was, she hoped, the final step in gaining complete control of the home world.

Poor Zack had wanted nothing to do with the post, happy just being constable and administrator of the Glaive. He knew everything about the Glaive, how it worked both within and without, the stated and underlying goals of its leader. He knew but did not fully understand many things, trusting and believing in Iroshi not to mislead him.

His acceptance speech was short, mostly a thank-you to everyone with whom he had worked and an expression of hope that the spirit of cooperation would continue. He welcomed the new constable, Burton Landry, made a few lofty and vague promises, gave a final thank-you for their attendance, and the ceremony ended with another round of applause. Everyone shook hands with someone, each wanting to shake hands with Mitchell, as they filed into the adjoining banquet room for the official reception.

The guests made their way to the bar, fully stocked with all kinds of alcoholic delights and various exotic beverages. She noted with satisfaction that each Glaive member accepted one of the many teas. Drinking liquor of any kind was forbidden in mixed company, that is, Glaive and non-Glaive. As the afternoon wore on they would pay their respects to Iroshi and the new governor, then gradually disappear, returning to their far-flung posts.

She stood apart now, watching. So many things had happened in the past eight years. A faster interstellar drive had reduced travel time from one star system to another by more than one-fourth, the one change that had allowed so many of her people to return for the ceremony.

In that time, the old temple had been rebuilt. The Glaive was now worth ten times the value of Mushimo's credit disc and the Nevan treasure combined, and was known on every world inhabited by her kind. The ancient scrolls had been translated, thanks to Ensi and the others.

Lucas approached and bowed. He was one of the few who was both warrior and truth-sayer.

"You're off?"

"Yes," he answered. "Lord Tago needs me at his side to strengthen his resolve."

"The marriage is arranged?"

"Very nearly. Just a few minor details to iron out, like which palace the happy couple will honeymoon in. Once everything's decided, the two kingdoms will be joined. Tago seems very pleased with it all."

"I am glad I found you, Lucas," she said earnestly. It had been a long search, four of those eight years.

"So am I." He smiled and bowed again. She walked with him to the door to say farewell.

Over the next hour she said goodbye to all the others going to their assignments. She wished that she could leave too, not being particularly fond of official functions, and experiencing one of those moments when she missed being on assignment like in the beginning. Mitchell also wished he was somewhere else. His posture showed his discomfort in the stiff, shiny new uniform. Had he for one moment thought he had to wear the thing all the time, there would have been no way to convince him to take the appointment.

She noted, uncomfortably, the approach of Robert Behrenstein, Commissioner of Guilds. He was too close for her to gracefully escape. She sighed mentally. At least now she might discover why he had come for this particular ceremony. The boy accompanying him looked gloomy, more than likely realizing that his time of coddling would soon end, if all stories were true.

"Iroshi, my dear. Another beautiful coup."

Behrenstein waved his hand foppishly at the entire room.

"It appears that the world is at last under your complete control."

"As much as is possible," she replied casually.

"Don't be so modest. Who in the galaxy can gainsay anything you choose to do?" He was baiting her, but why?

"Why, you, sir, the Council, the governor, and of course the constable."

She nodded toward a group of men that included the Council's envoy, Tesser Jasson, who had conducted the ceremony and delivered the necessary documents.

"What brought you so far out? Surely not such an insignificant world as ours."

"You are too modest. Even though you are at the farthest edge of the empire, Rune is one of the most well known of the worlds these days because of your Glaive." He fondled the boy's neck. "I've been dying to see what it was like here."

"Excuse me, Iroshi," Mitchell cut in, to her surprise and relief. He bowed to the commissioner and turned back to her. "Your attention is needed."

"I will see you later," she said to Behrenstein.

"Of course." He smiled, but the boy winced in pain as his mentor turned him away.

"Thanks," she said to Mitchell as they moved off. "As much as I would like to know why he is here, I don't think I could have stood him a moment longer. Someone else will find it out." Then, thoughtfully, she added, "Are we still working on him?"

"Yes. Other than his sexual preference and heavy drinking, there's nothing concrete yet. We do have a few more trails to follow."

"Good. He must either be destroyed or forced to work with us. I still believe his boys may be the key."

"We've been concentrating on that angle, as you suggested. Nothing has developed yet."

"He's a mean one. It seems none of his young lovers has ever stayed around for much more than six months. This current liaison has gone on for about four months and has all the appearances of coming to an end."

"We'll keep on it."

Mitchell looked around, making sure no one was within hearing. "I just found out something from Jasson I thought you might find interesting."

The envoy had his back to them.

"So, you were not just rescuing me."

Mitchell grinned.

"No, but I told Jasson I was. He seemed to understand completely." His grin faded.

"Anyway, he said that the Council is considering moving their headquarters from Earth."

"We have heard that rumor before."

"This time they're very serious. Teams have been sent out to investigate the possible new sites. It could be one reason for Behrenstein's being here."

"You mean they might be considering Rune-Nevas?"
"Yes."

As the air car circled the temple complex, Iroshi's mind turned from dark thoughts to memories. The open area of the courtyard was larger now than when it was filled with funeral pyres. It had been enlarged to accommodate the numerous air cars that came and went all day and night. Still, every time she flew in, memories returned of that night of fire she had experienced vicariously. As did the nagging doubt that the complex had not been restored to its former glory, in spite of Ensi's frequent assurances.

The driver guided the vehicle to the paved surface. He jumped out of the front seat, only to find she was out and moving away. She patted his shoulder in passing and left the door open for him to close.

Iroshi felt little patience for procedures, even those she had initiated herself, and barely returned the salute of the guard at the entrance to her building. The place was much changed from the time she slept on the sand in a sleeping bag on the first floor. Now her bed was on a brand-new third floor. The rest of the building contained offices, meeting rooms, and work space for her personal staff.

There were no messages waiting on the uncluttered desk. She started up the stairs to the meditation chamber on the third floor. Once she was inside, no one would disturb her unless there was a disaster.

"Ensi, is there anything needing immediate attention?"
No. Nothing.
"Good."

She closed the door and turned on the muted, indirect light. She peeled off her high boots, dropping them beside the door, and padded barefoot across the deep carpet to the round chaise in the center of the room. Although it was large enough for her to lie flat on, she pushed the loose pillows to the back and leaned against them. The only other item in the room was a refrigerator unit stocked with drinks

and a few food items for those times when she remained
here for hours working on a single problem.

"What about Mushimo?" she asked as she got comfortable.

I am here, Laicy.

His voice had the usual soothing effect on her nerves.
She did feel a sudden twinge of guilt that they only called
on him when there was a crisis, but the energy used in communicating across such distances should not be wasted on
things of little importance.

*Ensi has told me the problem. I was not entirely unaware
of the possibility of a move, but I had heard nothing about
Rune-Nevas in that connection.*

"It had never occurred to me. Behrenstein must have
been here for that reason.

"Dammit, we need more time. I don't think we are strong
enough yet to keep the Council from moving here if they
want to. Once they got here, we could not keep from being
swallowed up in their bureaucracy. If we fight them on either ground, and lose, we will never regain the lost prestige.

"Why would they want to come all the way out here?
This is the last outpost, so far from the center of the empire
that communication would be dangerously slowed. How
could they hope to control it all?"

Earth is the centermost world, of course, Ensi broke in.
*But the world itself has no other practical importance. It
has nearly become a backwater, a used-up world. No one
visits there, except on official business with the Council.*

Or to visit for sentimental reasons, Mushimo added.

"That is a reason for their leaving Earth. But it does not
explain why they would want to come here."

In part it does, Mushimo said. *If the Council were located on the same world as one of the strongest guilds, or
one of the largest corporations, some of the prestige would
reflect on them. If it could, in turn, control that organization one day, either directly or indirectly . . .*

Iroshi could almost see the familiar shrug.

The growing reputation of the Guild of the Glaive could be an enormous asset to them. Today, they're being looked on as a symbol of impotence. Then too, the very work of the Glaive would be an asset. Our warriors could be obligated to afford them protection. Perhaps they would tie up most of the truth-sayers on their business.

The Council members probably realize that the Glaive is growing stronger and will be even stronger in years to come, and if we should reach our full potential independently, what is left of their power will be seriously damaged. Perhaps lost completely.

"Their purpose, then, would be to increase their own standing at the expense of the Glaive's."

Yes. It would seem so.

Remember, each member of the Council is under the control of some organization or another. If they can find a single base of power and shake off the influence of their sponsors, the Council might once again be a powerful organization in its own right.

"But there is the danger of their being swallowed up by a single sponsor, of all the power and authority being concentrated under one influence."

Of course.

"We must protect our autonomy and objectivity. Our usefulness to our clients would be lost if we were too closely associated with the Council.

"At the same time we must keep the Council from being taken over by someone else. If they move, they could destroy the one thing they seek: their independence. The one thing we want them to have. The Council must be made stronger and more honest."

She opened her eyes and scooted off the chaise to pace the small open area between it and the walls. Other Glaive members had similar rooms within the complex, smaller than hers, in which no one was allowed except the person to whom it belonged. In these rooms they communed with their companions, bonding with them, learning to work together, and learning to establish the separateness required to maintain sanity. Each bonded pair, host and companion, established their own basic rules.

Iroshi returned to the chaise.

"I am not going to lose what has been built here, or what we have accomplished in the rest of the empire.

"We need some reason, some way, for Earth to gain in importance. Something to make the councilors want to remain headquartered there."

It is quite simple, Ensi said.

"What is?"

We give them all the benefits they think they would have by moving here.

"How?"

Establish a second temple on Earth. A small one, using any excuse: we need to be closer to our clients in that sector. We want the prestige of a base on man's home planet and of being closer to the Council.

You have a friend on Earth, and two of the companions are already there: Mushimo and Fotey. You could take a trip to Earth with no stated purpose, except to visit, but let the real reason leak out. Or you could state the purpose right up front. Of course, you may want to hold back until we are sure there is a problem.

Ensi and Mushimo withdrew so that Iroshi could consider the possibility of such a visit on her own. The most disturbing thought was the prospect of seeing Crowell again. There had been no communication between them since leaving Siebeling; her choice, of course, because he had not known where to get in touch with her. When she left him, she was convinced she was in love with him. But had he loved her? Would he now, if he found out she was Iroshi? She shook her head, driving these thoughts to the outer limits of her mind, to be considered later.

What was of immediate importance was the protection of the Glaive and its integrity. The idea of its presence on

Earth was a good one. But there was another reason, just as good.

"Mushimo, is Crowell still operating your dojo?"

Yes.

"Excellent. That will be our reason for visiting Earth and our continued presence there. Nira will be trained in Crowell's school."

Nira? Do you think it wise to uproot the child?

The child, Nira, was twelve years old and had been found in the streets of Kharta, the largest city on Vesta, a major mining world. Living in the streets and alleys, fending for herself, made her more mature than her years. Tyra, a warrior, found her two years ago while on an assignment and, knowing Iroshi's plan to train some children as warriors, had brought the girl with her when she returned.

During the first year Nira was examined and tested, much without her knowledge, and given training in the fighting skills each member needed. Her mind and personality were delicately probed by Ensi and others, all to ensure she was suited to assume the rigors of being a warrior or truth-sayer. In all ways she seemed infinitely suited and her companion, the sixty-third and last, was introduced to her. She accepted the presence with unexpected ease.

"If we explain to her truthfully and reasonably why the move is necessary," Iroshi answered. "She is strong and eager to learn. What better place for her to be taught than in the same dojo where I learned so much? Crowell"—she swallowed hard—"is a good teacher."

There were a few misgivings, but after discussion of all the possibilities they agreed to pursue that course. If Nira's experience there was good, perhaps all the children initiated into the Glaive would be trained there. Final arrangements would be worked out later. For now, Iroshi's visit to Earth must be planned.

At last Iroshi made her way to bed. It was early morning, and she needed a couple of hours' sleep before the ceremonial choosing by one of the newest warriors. She slipped under the covers. Mitchell turned over, wrapping his arms around her.

Iroshi pushed open the double doors and stood on the threshold for a moment with the young warrior. Inside stood racks of weapons, most of them swords. The collection grew every year, but still was less than half of what Mushimo had shown her all those years ago. With her hand she motioned for the young woman to enter.

"Choose your sword, Sheera."

"Any of them?" She spoke in a whisper, as most of them did at this moment.

"Any one."

Slowly Sheera stepped into the room. She had not gone far when she turned and looked at Iroshi, a puzzled expression on her face.

She hears, Iroshi thought, and nodded encouragement.

She inspected rack after rack while Iroshi remembered her own choosing. Sheera stopped before one of several ornately decorated scabbards, lifted one from its place and slowly returned to the door. Standing before her leader, still just inside the threshold, Sheera drew the blade. Iroshi nodded, and the new warrior slid the sword back into its sheath. She left the room to stand beside Iroshi once again as the doors closed.

10

The Journey

Nothing but blackness showed through the single window, essentially the same blackness that had appeared for nearly four weeks. The new interstellar drive may have cut travel time considerably, but it still took eight weeks to get from Rune-Nevas to Earth. Too long.

Traveling had never bothered her before; why was she tense this time? Granted, the racer was smaller than a liner, but this wasn't the first time she had been on one for an extended trip. It was large enough to accommodate Iroshi and her companions comfortably. She could discuss Glaive business with the staff through Ensi. There was plenty of room in her cabin to practice. There was more than enough quiet for reading and meditation.

Yet she was restless to the point of distraction. The kind of restlessness when things happen and she can do absolutely nothing to change them. Ensi was no help, experiencing his own sense of foreboding. He communicated with Mushimo, who knew of nothing impending. No one in the temple complex or on assignment had anything of great moment to report.

Iroshi jumped at the knock on the door and took a moment to compose herself before answering: breathe deeply, assume a relaxed posture on the sofa.

"Come in," she called.

Captain Ferguson entered, a pained look on his face. He bowed formally, then seemed reluctant to speak.

"Well?" she demanded.

"There is a problem . . ." He cleared his throat. "The navigator has become ill."

"The navigator?" she snapped, then forced herself to relax again, sit back on the sofa. "What's wrong with him?" More gently.

"We're not sure." He relaxed slightly. "It came on suddenly. Stomach cramps. Dizziness. Fever. He says he can get us as far as Amber. That's a small planetoid used as a way station for freighters. It has repair facilities for damaged ships."

"If we make it to this place . . . Amber?" He nodded. "How long will we need to be there? Will Thomas be able to continue in a short time? And if not . . ."

"There are always navigators on Amber looking for work. We could pick up a replacement there. Or, if not, one of the Glaive's navigators could be sent for, if close by."

She thought a moment.

"Once we get there, we will look at all the options and determine which will get us on our way fastest. The first thing is to get Thomas taken care of. Is there a doctor?"

He nodded.

"Good. Let the station know we are coming and what we need. Captain." He turned back from the door. "Thank you."

A smile flickered at the corners of his mouth as he bowed and left the cabin. Iroshi sat still, making a mental note to always keep in mind the dignity of men such as Ferguson. He had been captain of her personal racer all three years she had possessed it. He kept a respectful distance between them, where she would have fostered more of a friendship. She liked him, and somewhere in their relationship she had gotten the impression that he at least respected her. He was a man who always knew what he was doing. It would be tragic to lose the loyalty of anyone of his caliber.

But other matters needed attention.

"Ensi."

Yes.

"The navigator?"

It is difficult to tell. His symptoms could mean poison.

"Can you enter?"

No. It is taking every bit of his concentration to keep the racer on course and to keep the illness from affecting the performance of the ship. It would be too distracting.

It took nearly a full day to reach Amber, which was quite a feat for Thomas according to both the captain and Ensi. As a medical team took Thomas in charge, she instructed the doctor to inform her of his diagnosis.

A suite of rooms was put at their disposal for as long as they would need them. The racer was put under security seal as soon as everyone disembarked. A detector beam scanned them as they passed from hangar to lobby. No guns of any kind were allowed, since a puncture of the outer walls would allow the poisonous atmosphere to enter the complex. That safety rule was enforced on many worlds for similar reasons. On way stations like Amber, every sort of safety device was installed, authorities preferring prevention to cure, a most important policy where diverse cultures and professions mingled.

Thanks to Ferguson's advance warning, no guns were carried from the racer and they passed through the detectors without incident. Nothing was said about their swords.

A port official waited in the lobby, ready to act as guide. In keeping with her hope to leave soon, Iroshi declined the offer of a tour, wanting only to get to the rooms and start working on the possibility of replacing the navigator. If it had been allowed, she would have stayed on the racer, but that was another of the station's rules. It probably wouldn't hurt the lot of them to get out of the confines of the ship for a time anyway, she rationalized.

The engineer and first officer were shown to quarters near the hangar at Ferguson's request. He felt it wise to have someone close to the racer when in relatively unknown territory. Given the prevailing mood, both Ensi and Iroshi agreed.

The station was large, with a surprising degree of sophistication and comfort. Within the suite, Iroshi, Ferguson and Sheera had separate rooms. McCue, the steward, and Angie, the cook, shared a room, as was their habit. In some ways, Ferguson would have preferred to stay with the engineer and first officer, but it was his responsibility to aid in the search for another navigator, assuming Thomas would not recover soon.

The captain was the only one familiar with Amber. He was also experienced in detecting electronic devices, none of which he found in the rooms.

As the steward unpacked her case, Iroshi joined Sheera in her room. She bowed as Iroshi entered.

"I will leave you to your unpacking in a moment," she said, sitting in the only chair. She motioned for the young warrior to sit on the bed close to her.

"I brought you with us on this trip to give you a first taste of an assignment. It is proving to be a little more unpredictable than any of us expected.

"Settle in quickly, then have Lorin conduct a search for the nearest of our racers. We may need a replacement navigator, and if calling for one of our own is the quickest course, that is what we will do."

Sheera nodded her understanding, and Iroshi rose to leave. Her hand moved from the door control before it opened.

"Sheera," she said as she turned back. "Keep your sword close. There may be trouble."

"I've sensed tension for some time," she said.

"Good."

This trip might prove to be quite a test for the youngster, Iroshi thought as she passed through the sitting room. The warning may have been unnecessary, since everyone was alerted by recent events, but Sheera was new to all this.

As a child she had begun training in the martial arts but had never regarded the activity as anything more than a sport, unlike the older warriors and truth-sayers, many of whom were seasoned fighters before joining the Glaive.

Those others had wandered the worlds of man seeking combat experience and reputation, as ronin or mercenary. There were few warriors left in the empire, and future initiates would be young and inexperienced like Sheera, or children to be molded like Nira.

The steward was gone from the room when she entered. Everything had been put away, the swords arranged on the dresser top. A pitcher of tea waited on the small table. She sat in the chair and removed her knee-high boots. She stood and stripped off the blue uniform of belted cossack tunic and full trousers; then, in camisole and panties, she stretched out on the bed. It was time to practice, but the listlessness she had felt on the racer was still with her.

A knock on the door, and she jerked awake.

"One moment," she called. She pulled a robe from the closet, quickly brushed her short brown hair with her fingers, and opened the door. The doctor stood just outside with the steward, waiting patiently.

"Dr. Matthews. Please come in."

"Thank you." He stepped in, taking the chair she indicated.

"How is Thomas?"

"He's out of danger and resting comfortably."

"Good."

"He *was* poisoned. A very slow-acting variety probably administered before you left Rune-Nevas. He was fortunate to make it this far, but we've managed to neutralize it. There will be some residual effects, but I think nothing permanent. He's still very weak and won't be able to leave the infirmary for at least three or four days. I understand you are in a hurry to resume your journey."

"Yes, we are, doctor. I'm very glad, though, that Thomas is going to be all right. Thank you for coming to tell me." She rose. "If he needs anything, let me or any of my staff know."

"Of course. There is the matter of . . ." He hesitated.

"The fee? Someone will come by your office a little later to make all the arrangements."

"Thank you." He bowed.

Strange man, she thought after he was gone. Seemed perfectly competent, but stuck out here? She took off the robe and hung it back in the closet. Standing in front of the full-length mirror, she stretched first with her arms held to the sides, then pulled straight overhead. She studied her reflection as she did warm-up exercises, stretching, posing, and wondering.

"I haven't changed much in fourteen years, I don't think. A little rounder in places. Hair's shorter, still light brown. Eyes still green. A few wrinkles around the corners. Still five-eight." She placed her hands on either side of her waist. "Hmmmm, a little rounder."

With a wave of her hand, dismissing both thought and reflection, she pulled on a jumpsuit and prepared to practice. There wasn't much open space, so she used the short sword. It was easy to lose herself in the movements, in the oneness with the sword and everything in the surrounding area. She wove a path around lamps, tables, chairs, rolled across the bed to crouch beside it. Unseen enemies sprang from the corners of her mind. She poised, attacked, defended. Another knock on the door broke the concentration. Sword still in hand, she opened the door.

"Sorry to interrupt, Iroshi," Sheera said. "Lorin has completed the search."

"Come in." She replaced the sword in its scabbard. "The nearest Glaive ship . . ."

"Is at least one week distant," Sheera finished.

"Damn." Iroshi hit the table with a flat hand. "Thomas will be in the infirmary at least three or four days." She thought for a moment. "Thank you, Sheera. Would you ask Captain Ferguson to come in?"

Sheera bowed and went to summon the captain. Iroshi

sat in the chair, staring at nothing in particular on the far wall.

"Ensi. Do you detect any specific problems?"

None. Will you wait for Thomas?

"Not if we can find a competent navigator to replace him. I want to be on our way quickly. This whole thing is taking on the flavor of a trap." Aloud she said, "Come in, Captain."

She told him what the doctor said.

"Have you found any navigators looking for work?"

"Yes. There are seven. One I know to be an alcoholic. A second has an unsavory reputation. That leaves five we can talk to."

"All right. Would you make arrangements for us to interview them, this evening if possible, after dinner?"

He nodded, then asked, "Anything else?"

"No. Right now I'm going to dress and go for some dinner. Join us there as soon as you finish."

He bowed and left on his errand.

She washed and, dressed again in the blue uniform, she told the steward to see the doctor and make payment for services rendered and enough to cover Thomas's needs for the duration of his stay. She slipped the katana and wakizashi through the wide sash, and she and Sheera left for the dining room. She wore only the chosen katana; the short sword was awarded to Glaive members after they proved themselves in combat.

The dining room proved smaller than expected but, after going through the line, they managed to find an isolated table. The other diners regarded them intently for several minutes, then returned to their own conversations. On the whole, they were a rather motley-looking group, about sixty diners she guessed, wondering how many were assigned to Amber and how many just passing through.

The food was barely palatable, and Sheera wondered aloud why they had not eaten the packaged food brought from the racer. Iroshi waved to Ferguson as he came through the line.

"You look pleased," she commented as he set the tray on the table and slipped into the chair.

"It's arranged for the navigators to start coming by about six this evening."

"All five?"

"Only four. One has suffered a breakdown and is just looking for passage home."

"That is not all that pleases you," she teased. He looked slightly embarrassed.

"No, it isn't." He took a sweeping look around the room. "It's being here, even sitting in this old-fashioned dining area and eating this horrible food. It reminds me of old times."

"When you were an independent?"

"Yes. It was exciting at times."

"Do you miss it?"

He thought a moment. "I miss being young enough to enjoy it."

He tapped the hilt of his saber. "We used to have some good times. But I'm content with what I'm doing now."

Iroshi nodded, then turned the conversation back to the navigators. Ferguson had heard of two of them, but not enough to form any advance opinion.

"You were a navigator once, were you not?"

He looked slightly uncomfortable.

"How did you know? Of course. You investigated my background thoroughly before offering me this job."

Iroshi nodded.

"Yeah. I was a navigator for a few years."

"Does my asking make you uncomfortable?"

"In most places people treat them like freaks. Navigators, I mean. Even former ones. We allow ourselves to be mutilated with surgical implants in our heads and then hooked up to a spaceship. When we're working, we *are* the ship, in almost every way. When we're not working, well, we're thinking about it. It . . . the job . . . becomes a big part of us. In the old days, with the old interstellar drives, we practically had to hold the ships together. The vibrations were terrific.

"We are comfortable only with other navigators because only our peers know how it is. The rest of society can't understand. If they don't persecute us, people just ignore us."

He stopped, embarrassed again, this time by his intensity and talkativeness.

"I have always wondered what it would be like," Iroshi said dreamily. "One day I am going to try it."

Ferguson and Sheera looked at her in surprise. She laughed.

"No, I am not crazy. But right now we had better get back so we can be ready for the first interview."

Laicy, hold!

She had just reached for the door control pad.

"What is it, Ensi?"

Ferguson looked at her strangely. She held up her hand, then pressed forefinger to lips. Sheera listened to her own inner voice.

There is someone inside, but I cannot tell how many. More than one.

"Are they in the sitting room?"

No. In the other rooms, waiting to surprise you once you are inside.

She examined the door. There was no way to open it without the *whish* it made when the control pad was pressed. They could not surprise the assassins except with their own preparedness. She opened the door and they entered quickly, taking positions just inside at her silent command.

Two ninja appeared in an instant from Sheera's room, one from Iroshi's, and one from the steward and cook's.

Sheera found herself facing the pair of masked warriors. Iroshi fought her attacker, slowly working her way toward

the young woman. She feinted with the katana to the head
of her adversary, whose sword came up. She changed the
direction of the blade to curve around, cutting off the man's
right hand at the wrist. She left him to his agony and turned
to aid Sheera, who was barely holding her own. Just as
Iroshi entered the battle, a figure appeared in the outer
doorway.

"What the hell . . ."

The voice touched a memory deep inside her. Concentration wavered for an instant.

Laicy! Ensi shouted from within.

The enemy saw the opening and struck swiftly.

She regained her momentum a moment too late as the
blade caught her left side. She moved slightly with the
stroke, enough to keep the edge from biting deeply. Pain
left her breathless. She dropped to her knees, waiting for
the finishing blow.

With a roar, the newcomer attacked the ninja from behind, beating him to the floor with a wooden club. Her vision blurred by pain, Iroshi crawled out of the way.
Ferguson saw her fall. His rage transferred to the saber and
he forced his opponent backward against the wall, where he
ran him through. Glancing to see that Sheera was in no immediate danger, he moved to Iroshi's side.

The stranger stood over the now still form of his adversary and all eyes turned to Sheera who, unaware of any of
them, had found her skill once the odds were even. An
opening came and she swung, catching the ninja in the side,
nearly cutting him in two. Sheera whirled around as the
man fell and, seeing there were no more enemies standing,
turned to look down at the broken body. Her breathing
came in ragged gulps after the exertion and excitement of
her first combat.

Ferguson tore open Iroshi's tunic and examined the
wound. She winced in pain, but her attention stayed with
Sheera. The young woman had done very well, but reaction
was setting in. The captain called the young woman's

name. Iroshi put her hand on his arm, shook her head. Ferguson nodded and went to the telecom himself, calling for the doctor and security.

Sheera's hand raised the sword until she could see the blade without moving her head. Blood was beginning to dry, forming rusty-looking spots on the sheen of steel. She lowered the sword, turned, faced Iroshi. Blankness faded from her eyes. Iroshi recognized the look of personal horror that replaced it. Sheera had killed a human being, and no amount of training could prepare anyone for that first time. To do it, yes. To cope with the feelings, no.

Sheera's gaze lowered. She saw blood running freely between Iroshi's fingers.

"My god, Iroshi. You're hurt."

She took a step forward, then changed direction for the bathroom. The slamming door blocked the sound of her sickness.

Ferguson closed the key for the telecom.

"Help me," he said to the stranger.

The two of them lifted Iroshi to the sofa. Through the pain, she studied the man. Did she really know him? After so many years of nothing, had he reappeared in her life? As he released her, she took hold of his arm.

"Thank you for your help."

His smile was like a wound across his weary face.

"Darnedest interview I've ever had."

That voice! She knew it. And she didn't want to.

"Captain Ferguson. Could you get our friend a drink?" Turning back to the stranger, she said, "If you don't mind waiting a little. Until we get things cleaned up. Then we can get to the real thing."

"Sure, I don't mind."

Ferguson handed him a large portion of something swirling darkly in a glass, and the navigator moved to a chair in a back corner of the room.

The bathroom door opened, and a pale Sheera returned. She knelt beside the sofa.

"I'm sorry, Iroshi."

"For what?"

"For my weakness."

"Do you think you are different from anyone else?" Iroshi asked kindly. With her free hand she raised Sheera's chin. She looked so young.

"Killing another human being for the first time, or killing anything, is one of the hardest things a man or woman sometimes has to do. If you reacted with any less humanity, I would not have you in the Glaive."

The young warrior smiled wanly but gratefully.

"Everyone reacts the same way?"

"Maybe not exactly. But with the same degree of disgust and sorrow."

Sheera raised her right hand to comb fingers through her curly blond hair. Iroshi took hold of her wrist and pulled it toward her.

"You have been cut."

She turned the hand so Sheera could see the crimson streak across the back.

"You had better tend to it."

The doctor entered at that moment with two assistants and four security men right behind. Ferguson supervised the removal of the dead and wounded ninja, and directed one of the assistants to the steward's room. While the doctor tended to Iroshi's wound, Ferguson explained to the head of security what had happened.

Dr. Matthews pronounced her lucky. Nothing vital was injured, only one rib cracked and a good amount of blood lost. He cleaned the wound, then closed it with artificial tissue and bound her ribs. As he gave her an injection to speed up the body's production of blood, a second navigator came to the door. Ferguson talked to him a moment and he left. Iroshi assumed he was given instructions to tell the others to come back tomorrow, or some such message, since no one else appeared.

Before long the room cleared as if by magic. One minute

it was full of people and activity, and the next nearly empty. After assuring herself that Iroshi was in no danger, Sheera went to her room. The cook, who was found unconscious in her bathroom, was put to bed with a slight concussion. The steward was dead. Arrangements for him would have to be made tomorrow. Sometime during the night the silent servo units would clean up most of the blood and litter.

Iroshi reclined on the sofa, feeling pale and tired. She thought of asking for a mirror to confirm the superficial diagnosis. However, there was something else to tend to, something she would prefer to delay. Ferguson sat in a nearby chair awaiting instructions.

"Well, Captain. Let's interview our navigator."

The man heard and moved to stand before the sofa.

"Are you sure you feel well enough?" Ferguson asked.

"Yes, Captain. Pull up a chair, sir," she said to the navigator. "It is late and I believe we are all tired."

"First, may we have your name?" Ferguson said as soon as he sat down.

"Jonathan Campbell."

"Father?" Iroshi whispered.

11

Reunions

Iroshi sat in the bed, propped up by pillows, the breakfast tray untouched. The wound in her side throbbed—the price for refusing the painkiller. She did not want to be made more helpless by its narcotic effect. In this case, a clear head meant no sleep. She would have tossed and turned all night if it had not been too painful to move.

Other pain nagged at her.

Why did he show up now? When her life and conditions for the Glaive were so tense, and the outcome of the next few weeks so very important. The power of the Glaive was about to face its first major test. Such a distraction as this was the last thing she needed.

The scene from last night came flooding through. She lay awash in feelings for a moment, then regained control, forcing them down. Handling them. She reached for the cube on the table, thumbed it on for perhaps the hundredth time. Her father in the projected image. Her father in the sitting room last night. Older, tired. Shocked to find out his daughter was Iroshi, founder of the Guild of the Glaive, warrior and confidante of some of the most important people. Known throughout the empire.

Both he and Ferguson had looked at her so strangely when she whispered that one word: father. They had looked at one another, as if to confirm they had heard correctly.

"What . . ." The navigator cleared his throat. "What did you say?"

Iroshi stared at him. Momentarily, old hatred surfaced. It faded into emotional shock, paralyzing her. Until the pain in her side penetrated her mind once again, forcing an opening to consciousness.

"Who are you?" Campbell asked.

"I am Iroshi," she answered huskily. "Of the Guild of the Glaive. I once *was* Laicy Campbell, born on Siebeling."

His face went white. His right hand shook as it extended toward her, stopping halfway when she cringed away.

"Laicy?" There were tears in his eyes. "So many years. So far away." His hand dropped to his lap.

Ferguson watched warily as the scene unfolded. It was his duty to protect Iroshi if necessary. At the moment he did not know if there was danger, but he was ready.

"Why did you leave us?" Her voice was heavy with spite.

Campbell bowed his head. "So many reasons," he muttered. "Some you should understand." His head came up.

"What do you mean?"

"You left Siebeling to find a life for yourself."

"But I didn't leave a wife and three children to fend for themselves!"

"Neither did I."

"You did!"

"Your mother didn't want me. As soon as I could, I sent credits for you children."

"You didn't. You couldn't."

They glared at each other.

"Get out," she shouted.

He jumped to his feet, toppling the chair. A new pain deepened the lines of his face as he turned for the door. Ferguson hastily followed him.

"Come back tomorrow," he said in a low voice as Campbell started out. "Late morning."

He could only hope Campbell would do as he said. Instinct told him that this confrontation must not be left hanging like this.

The captain arranged to have one of the medical assistants bathe Iroshi and get her to bed. She suffered through it all in complete silence, refused food and drink as well as the painkiller capsules. Alone in her room, she activated the cube for the first time that night, having gotten it from the bag sometime during the flurry of activity. It always went with her when she traveled. Why? Had she expected to find him one day? Now she had found him and had not reacted as she thought she would.

The image floated just above the bedcovers.

"Ensi?"

He had been "not there" during the whole scene.

Yes, Laicy.

"I don't think I want to cope with all this at one time."

If you put your father off until all else is resolved, you might lose him again.

"I'm not sure I care." She sounded petulant, like a child.

If you did not care, there would be no problem in dealing with it.

"Stop being so damned logical."

Too many crises. Emotional, professional situations getting out of hand. She couldn't remember feeling so confused, so overcome at any other time in her life.

"Ensi." No response. "Ensi!" She waited a moment.

"Please don't sulk. I am sorry I was sharp with you."

I do not sulk. Do you want my thoughts on the situation?

"Yes, please."

Take some time to talk with him. Get to know him. Give yourself time to sort out the feelings his presence has reawakened.

Let the other matters wait for your attention until you confront them directly. Your basic strategy is complete. Only small details are left to be worked out, and you cannot address them until you have more information.

Take him with you, perhaps as a relief navigator. Just in case.

"Have you scanned him?"

I surface-scanned him as a matter of course when he first appeared. Before I knew who he is. He is no immediate threat. Other than that, this is a personal matter, between the two of you, and I will go no further.

"All right. I will try to contact him later this morning. If he has not left the station."

She had not found the courage by the time Angie entered to retrieve the tray.

"Do you want me to take this?"

Iroshi nodded. "Are you feeling better this morning, Angie?"

"Oh, yes. A little headache, but that will go away soon, I'm sure."

"I am sorry about McCue."

She didn't know how close the cook had been to the steward, but they worked together for a long time.

"So am I." Tears appeared in the girl's eyes.

"Would you please ask Captain Ferguson to come in for a moment?"

"Certainly."

Perhaps she was too abrupt. Under other circumstances, she would have shown Angie more sympathy for what was clearly a loss to her. She would have talked to her for a time and offered comfort. Wouldn't she? But the time had come to act on her own problem.

Ferguson arrived. She put off the real reason for asking him to come.

"How is Thomas this morning?"

"Still uncomfortable but better."

"I am glad. What of the ninja warriors? I believe at least one was still alive when they were taken away."

"All dead. The wounded one—you cut off his hand—died during the night."

"Did he say anything?"

"Never regained consciousness."

"I had hoped we might learn something."

Ferguson nodded agreement. They sat in awkward silence.

"I guess I will leave the interviews to you," she said. "If you don't mind."

"I'll take care of it."

"I want to leave first thing in the morning, so that should be taken care of quickly."

He stood, bowed, and moved to the door.

"Captain," she said. He turned and waited. "Would you find my . . . Mr. Campbell . . . and ask him to come see me?"

"Of course."

He bowed again and left the room, feeling pleased with himself for anticipating the request. Of course, if Campbell did not come back on his own, Ferguson would have to look for him.

Any action on his part proved unnecessary. Just before eleven o'clock, Campbell knocked on the outer door. A minute later he was sitting in a chair next to Iroshi's bed. They sat uneasily, waiting for Ferguson to leave the room. Campbell stared at a spot on the edge of the bed. Iroshi looked down at her lap, surprised to find the remnants of a shredded paper napkin scattered about.

He cleared his throat, but she concentrated on gathering up the shreds. It proved to be more than a handful, and once she had it all accumulated she did not know what to do with it. Campbell held out his hands, and she carefully transferred the feathery bits. His hands felt warm and a little rough against her cold ones. He went to the disposal bin in the wall and dropped the mess into it. Only a few bits floated away into the room somewhere.

"Laicy," he said as he returned to the chair.

"Yes . . . Father?"

Their eyes met for the first time, but each looked away quickly.

"I never meant to hurt you or the boys. I have to admit I didn't give the three of you as much thought as I should. It wasn't that I didn't care about you. I did."

"Then what drove you into space and away from us?"

"A lot of things." He sighed. "I had to get away from Siebeling, and your mother. Both were killing me.

"The only way to make money there is in the mines. But it wasn't in me to do that kind of work. Couldn't bear the confinement. I was always restless. Always had the feeling that there was something, somewhere, meant just for me. There probably never was anything special, that I would be really good at, but I had to look for it, just in case."

He glanced sideways at her. Hope rose naked in his eyes, hope that she could understand. She would not look at him, kept her expression controlled. The hope flickered out.

"Your mother wouldn't move. She wanted to stay in that house, wanted me to work in the mines, get promoted, until we could afford a better one. I tried. For a lot of years. Then I found out she was . . . She said I wasn't a man, wasn't a miner. David isn't my son."

Iroshi's head jerked up, her tongue ready to call him a liar. But in his eyes she saw truth. She thought back.

Her mother had always acted so proper. But later, when there was more time, Iroshi would remember the little trinkets that suddenly appeared, and the way some of the men acted when they brought their laundry. Other little instances, barely remembered and of no significance, would lead to one simple conclusion. But later. She listened, and instinct accepted his words as truth. So far.

"None of that excuses your abandoning us."

Truth or not, she still felt angry and betrayed.

"I know," he admitted. "But I did everything I could to see that you were provided for. From the very beginning, or at least as soon as I was able, I sent Martha half of what I earned. I only stopped recently because I figured David is old enough now to be out working."

"That is what you said last night. But I don't believe it. We never had enough money. She and I washed laundry, and she worked in the mines herself."

"Every day? In the mines, I mean."

"No. She had one day off each week."

"Did you ever see her, either working or in a uniform?"

"No. She said the boss would not like it if we hung around, so we never went there. Her uniforms were kept in the locker. She changed there."

Had her mother ever said that about the uniforms or had she just assumed? Laicy wondered.

"Laicy, your mother isn't a bad person. I loved her very much at one time. But I never knew her. She was one who couldn't be satisfied, always wanting more. But she wasn't willing to take chances. Wanted everything given to her.

"The worst part is that I never got to know you either. Or the boys."

He got up, paced the room a moment. She watched him, truly seeing him.

He was probably around six feet tall, but he had become slightly stooped, his shoulders rounded, robbing him of several inches. He was thin, almost painfully so, and his face was careworn. Or was it only the passage of time that had lined that face? The hair was still full and blond, except where the implants gleamed metallically behind the left ear. He stopped pacing to stand at the foot of the bed.

"You must have felt much the same as I did. You left Siebeling in search of . . . what? Your destiny? Looking at you, even if I didn't know who you have become, I can't imagine your living back there. A miner or the wife of a miner. Or perhaps some lowly government official. You wouldn't have settled for such a life. You were luckier than me, because you realized that before you accepted the first thing that was offered."

She softened slightly. He was right, of course. Such a life would not have held her. She motioned to the chair.

"Tell me about your life, what you have been doing all these years. Help me understand."

A look of relief came across his face. He smiled and sat back down. For the next two hours he talked about the things he had done, the places he had seen.

He left Siebeling as a crewman on a freighter, handling

the loading and unloading. He had quickly worked his way up to foreman, and after saving up the tuition, he went to school to become an astronavigator, as navigators were officially called. A year of school and then apprenticeship. Ten years ago he had taken his first solo.

From the tone of voice, the way he described each trip as an adventure, she could tell he enjoyed being a navigator. Most of all he loved the wonder of being one with the ship, a quality she had seen in others of his profession.

She stifled a yawn.

"You must be getting tired. We can talk again later."

"Yes," she said, then winced in pain as she shifted her pillow. "The loss of blood and all has left me a bit weak.

"I do want to talk with you some more, but we are leaving in the morning. Will you come with us?"

"If you're offering me the job as navigator, the answer is no." There was determination in his voice.

"Why?" She felt suddenly wary again.

"I can't be your navigator. I wasn't here on Amber by accident. I was told to try to hire on as your navigator if you made it this far."

"By whom?"

"An agent for the navigators' guild. He's gotten me assignments before."

"What were you supposed to do if you got the job?"

"Just make sure you didn't get to Earth for an extra week. I don't know why."

"I have a good idea," she said tightly. "Why didn't you tell me this before?"

"To be honest, I forgot for a time, finding out who you are and all. Then I figured it wasn't necessary. You wouldn't hire me as your navigator, and you'd go off and leave me sitting here. Besides . . ." He paused. "I owe some people."

"Like the agent?"

"For one."

"I have to get to Earth soon, and I cannot wait here any

longer. Come with me, and we will sort all this out during the trip."

He regarded her a moment before speaking.

"You think you can trust me?"

She nodded.

"Okay," he said at last.

The short walk from the suite to the racer had been more exhausting than she had thought possible. But it had been important that everyone see her leave on her own two feet, putting to rest any negative stories that might be circulating about her condition.

The racer lifted as soon as possible and the trip to Earth resumed. Iroshi spent the next two days in her cabin, recuperating, talking to her father, and thinking.

"Ensi, this is no longer just personal. Will you scan him, please? Just so we know where the danger might lie and that my father is not involved any further than we know about."

Yes. That I can and will do.

"Good. I will need to know as soon as possible. I would also like to know when the Council is planning a vote on the move. Very soon, I would think. Contact Mushimo and see if he can find out anything."

It turned out that Campbell had told the truth and that nothing could be learned about the vote. The Council was being unusually tight-lipped on the subject, but ways would be found to get the information. A direct probe was ruled out for the moment as being just slightly too direct.

Iroshi's spirit recuperated before her body, and the inactivity became trying. The conversations with her father helped to alleviate her restlessness, as he also came to depend on them. As a navigator, he had little freedom when on board ship. What little he did have was always wasted time. There was nothing to do for a man who was looked upon as a necessary freak by most others, even his shipmates. If not for her, he would have roamed the decks aimlessly.

He told her that he had done some things about which he was not particularly proud, just as she had. His philosophy was not to dwell on them. Nothing could change them, and most of those doors of his life were closed, emotionally. Except for his children, about whom he felt an honest guilt.

Like most navigators, he was apolitical, caring little for events outside of the ships he guided through the blackness between worlds. Unlike Captain Ferguson, he had no desire for any other career, convinced that he had found, if not the special place he had sought, at least the one in which he belonged.

In turn she told him of her life, the public version, hinting that there was more so he wouldn't be surprised later if she decided to tell all. She skimmed over the years of the quest, describing her travels as a restless search for her own niche. She concentrated on the events following her arrival on Rune. He was very interested in the Glaive and its goals.

Four weeks can become a very long time, and they were quickly talked out. A friendship was growing, which, given time and care, could become lasting and supportive. She toyed with the idea of offering him a permanent job as navigator on one of the racers so that he would not be lost to her again, but decided to wait.

Before leaving Amber, Iroshi had decided to leave Sheera with Thomas just in case he might be placed in danger again. Lucas would pick them up on his way to Earth to join her. That meant, however, that there was no one with whom to practice, something she missed very much.

As they neared orbit around Earth, Iroshi's thoughts turned more and more to the reunion still ahead. A reunion with Crowell, about whom she knew very little since their separation. The first man she had loved, both physically and emotionally. Did he know she and Laicy Campbell were the same person? Probably not, although he might have guessed.

Did he like what he heard about Iroshi? Again, probably not.

As the day of landing drew nearer she became more apprehensive, sharp-tongued with her companions.

Earth appeared at last. As they landed, Ferguson informed her that a crowd had gathered in the terminal and an enclosed air car was standing by at the platform to take her to Crowell. He had made the plans for getting her out of the port, and she was on her way in a matter of minutes. Captain Ferguson remained behind to handle all the paperwork and would join her later. Campbell also stayed behind, but only after promising to come with Ferguson.

The air car left the city behind. Below was a countryside, seemingly peaceful. Soon, she spotted the buildings in the distance, so familiar, even seeing them from above for the first time.

The car spiraled downward. Standing just outside the gate were two men whom she recognized immediately. The tall one was Crowell. Beside him stood Akiro. They came forward to greet her as the car set down in the grass. She swallowed hard and stepped out.

Akiro smiled a warm welcome. Crowell held a formal attitude. Time had changed her a little and dimmed the memories. The official uniform did not help. She took off her hat and stepped forward. A sudden look of recognition came over Crowell's face, and he stiffened even more. Color drained from his face, then rushed back, turning his face crimson.

"Laicy!"

"Hello, Crowell."

The room was the same. During the next few weeks, when her mind wandered, she would sometimes believe that she was nineteen again and Mushimo waited in the garden to share breakfast or dinner.

Crowell maintained the custom of eating outside, reinforcing the feeling of familiarity. The differences were often hard to bear, such as the large number of students in the school. Most of them were Terran, perhaps three being from the colonies.

There was also a larger staff to handle the needs of the students. Akiro was no longer a servant (although she wondered if he ever had been) but a full-time teacher. He had aged visibly, and seeing him changed had added to her sadness. He, on the other hand, was genuinely happy to see her, and to have the opportunity to talk about the old days, and the old master.

Was Crowell happy to see her? Shocked was more like it. So much so that she was glad no plans had been made for that first day, giving them the chance to get reacquainted. She looked forward to it with both apprehension and gladness.

They excused themselves right after introductions were made and went into the study. She sat down but Crowell paced, working out his feelings physically and verbally.

"Why didn't you tell me you are Iroshi?"

He had stopped pacing long enough to fling the words at her.

"You never suspected?"

"The possibility crossed my mind. You were the only woman I knew who could fight like that. But that didn't mean there couldn't be others. Then, as more details drifted about, I decided it couldn't be you doing those things. I still can't believe it."

"Much of it is true."

"You? You picked fights and killed people so you could establish a reputation?"

"Sometimes. To establish a reputation, but more to gain experience. But always with experienced warriors. I had to find the void. Mushimo had found it, you had found it. It was part of my quest.

"Please sit down. Looking up at you is hard on my neck."

He fell into a large chair next to her. Only once before had she seen him this agitated, back on Siebeling.

"I did not tell you about Iroshi because in some ways I was ashamed," she said after a time. "Your opinion has always mattered to me, and I could not bear the thought of your disapproval.

"At the same time, I knew you had your own problems to handle. Coming back here, given the circumstances, must have been extremely difficult. After a time, it seemed that our destinies were completely separate. The only way I could help you, or so it seemed, was to keep my problems to myself.

"Until now."

He seemed to have recovered from the initial shock and was much calmer. For that she was grateful.

"I don't think I am bringing you any of my problems. At least not directly. The Glaive has initiated its first child, an orphan. Nira will need the best training. That means starting here, Mushimo's way, if you agree. She can read and write and do basic mathematics."

"Does she want to learn kendo and other martial arts? Even more important, does she want to be a member of your Glaive?"

"She is not entirely sure yet. She is, after all, only twelve years old. She will have the option of leaving us if she should truly want to. But she has shown a real skill with the sword, and an eagerness to learn."

"And you came all this way to see if I would take her on as a student?"

Iroshi nodded.

"If it works well with Nira, we would like to use your school, your skills, as part of the training for all of our future warriors. We would not want to take up your entire school. There probably will not be that many initiates at any one time, anyway.

"Such an arrangement would also give us a base here on Earth. Where we can keep an eye on the Council."

"Which is the real reason you are here."

She smiled.

"What is the Glaive really going to do?" he asked, not smiling back.

"There is a strong push within the Council to move their headquarters to Rune-Nevas. Their very presence there would be a threat to the autonomy of the Glaive, and I will not have our integrity compromised in such a way. Nor will I have the Glaive become embroiled in their affairs. Not as their tool.

"The use of your school is a real desire on my part, but it also makes a good excuse to be here now to try to dissuade the members of the Council from such a move. We understand the decision is to be made soon."

"That part of your plan might prove more difficult than you think."

"Why?"

She feared he might refuse to consider her offer.

"Because one of Mushimo's sons is a member of the Council. And he despises me."

12

Crowell's Return

Crowell told his own story from his arrival at the terminal. Akiro met him there. It had been such a long time, and Crowell was feeling such mixed emotions. He wanted first to take time to deal with those feelings, but Mushimo's lawyers insisted on seeing him immediately. Perhaps it was just as well to get the mundane things out of the way as quickly as possible.

That was not to be either. He had little experience dealing with lawyers or legal matters and was ill-prepared for the gyrations necessary to get all the problems resolved, the questions answered. This particular case proved to be even more difficult than normal.

It was in this first meeting that he learned what neither he nor Laicy had suspected. Mushimo had two sons who were alive, living near Tokyo, and not particularly happy about being deprived of what they viewed as their rightful inheritance. The two had made themselves known just a few days after Crowell was notified of the terms of the will.

Mushimo must have known what his sons might do, for he made separate provisions for giving Crowell a credit disc, similar to the arrangement he had made for Laicy. Also, his home and dojo had been signed over to Crowell a number of years earlier without the latter's knowledge. At least he had a roof over his head, and the means with which to keep it there and to fight for his bequest. Both were given to him at that same meeting.

A whole week after arriving, and hours after the final

meeting, he and Akiro set out for the complex in one of the new air cars that Akiro had purchased for Crowell's use.

Crowell took a slow breath and settled deeper into the seat. He remembered the driver as one of Mushimo's servants. Akiro sat next to Crowell, calmly watching the scenery pass beneath.

If Crowell's feelings had been mixed before, they were in turmoil at that point. He had walked into a hornet's nest with blinders on, and did not like it one bit. He let his gaze drift off into the distance as twilight set in.

"Akiro, did you know about his sons?"

"Yes."

"Why didn't you tell me? I might have been better prepared for this."

"The master forbade any mention of them for as long as he lived. Their very existence brought him only shame. Several times he thought to destroy them, but they were too well protected. In the end it was he who was destroyed."

"Are you saying they killed him?"

"Yes. The ninja who attacked him while Laicy was here—she told you?—were sent by them."

"She and I were attacked on Siebeling just after the communication disc came about the will."

"I did not know that. Probably sent by them also."

"Why exactly did they kill him? I mean, they must have known Mushimo had disowned them."

"He was a threat to them. Always was. If they could kill him, they could also kill his successor. Once they knew who it was."

Akiro stretched to look a little farther ahead.

"We will land now. We can finish our talk in the study. Do not be alarmed by the number of armed warriors in the compound. I have hired several guards for your protection and the protection of the household."

Crowell nodded, alert as they settled to earth. He stepped into the darkness just outside of the gate. Before anything else, he had to meet the members of the household who were assembled in the main hall. With his consent, Akiro requested a light dinner be served in the study. Then he was shown to his room to freshen up. He had feared they might want to put him in the master's room, but it turned out to be one he had never slept in before. All the rooms were similar, but it was still a relief nevertheless that it was an unfamiliar one.

Akiro was pouring tea when Crowell entered the study. They ate together silently. Crowell was not particularly hungry, but his appetite quickened at the nearly forgotten taste of real Earth food. If only everything could be so pleasant, he thought as he settled back in the chair.

"Akiro, you didn't completely answer my questions before. Why didn't you tell anyone about Mushimo's sons after he died? By the way, what are their names?"

"Ozawa and Toshiro. I did not tell you at the express order of the master. He feared you would not claim the inheritance if you knew there were sons."

Crowell nodded. He still might not.

"He was determined they would not possess what they had turned their backs on."

"What happened to turn them against one another?" Crowell asked. He poured them another cup of tea.

"The master had traveled for nearly ten years, seeking knowledge, adding to his skills as a warrior with other techniques. When he left Earth he left behind an expectant wife and two-year-old son. When he returned there was a second son.

"He also found a wife full of resentment at being left on her own for so long. She had two sons to look after and had been forced to live without the comfort of a man's love.

"Mushimo loved them all a great deal, and he tried to make it up to them. All those years he had been gone. He taught those boys kendo and other martial arts and the honor of the old ways, his way. It was not to be their way, for he had been gone too long. Ozawa was wild, always scheming. Toshiro was a good kendo student, but he had been patterning his life after his older brother.

"Earth was, and is, an unruly place. All kinds of illegal and immoral practices and trades have their sources here. Ozawa was attracted to the people who controlled such businesses. Toshiro worshipped his brother. He followed into the depths of the crime world.

"Ozawa was cunning and ruthless and worked his way up in the hierarchy of his chosen field. Toshiro, with his fighting skills, became very useful in the training of a small army. As if he knew such skills were more suited to their kind of business, Toshiro chose the ways of the ancient ninja, ninjitsu. The practice had disappeared about four hundred years before.

"The master disowned them, banned them from his home and school. His wife died soon after that. Several times over the next years, the brothers sent the ninja to assassinate their father; then Ozawa became head of his organization. For twenty years there was peace of a sort. As if they had all they needed."

Akiro sipped his tea. He concentrated on the movement as if it were an anchor in the present.

"The master was able to concentrate on teaching after that. There were times when he could forget the bitterness of such sons, especially when a special student came to the dojo. Such a one was Laicy."

He noticed the look on Crowell's face but misunderstood its meaning.

"You were also special to him. That is made clear by his bequest. But your strengths were different. To him, Laicy was the true classical warrior. She had superb natural skills that were being honed to near perfection. Her psychic abilities were above the ordinary, although she was not totally aware of them. The strongest indication came when the sword chose her and she chose it. She did not know why.

"Her one fault is too strong a will. She also is impatient. She seeks the void, pursues it, rather than allowing it to find her, gradually. Until she learns to be more flexible, such goals will elude her. Only then will she reach her full potential."

Crowell nodded.

"I thought we would never find the one Mushimo sought until Laicy came along," Crowell said. "Of the two I sent to him, she was the one I was surest of." He turned the cup in his hand.

"I never have been entirely sure what Mushimo was looking for or why."

"He often praised your good sense in recognizing her uniqueness."

Crowell recognized the evasion but let it pass.

"And now she's gone from us."

Akiro studied him for a moment as Crowell became lost in other memories.

"How, then, did Mushimo die?" he asked.

"He was practicing in the back garden. There were no students. Laicy had only recently left, of course. I was in here doing some work. Suddenly I sensed something was wrong. I went looking for him. It took a while. He was lying near a hedge. He had been shot with an arrow and died instantly.

"The officials and I managed to suppress the real cause of death, saying it was his heart. He was one hundred thirteen years old and had become frail. Especially after Laicy left.

"Anyway, people believed the story readily enough."

"He was how old?"

"One hundred thirteen."

"I don't believe it. How old are his sons?"

"Ozawa is seventy-eight and Toshiro is seventy-five. I am seventy-six," he added. "We live much longer lives here on Earth. We haven't the stresses of the colonies. The atmosphere is much more healthful than it was two or three hundred years ago, when the population was higher.

"Politicians and criminals are the exceptions, of course. They kill each other off with astonishing regularity."

Papers lay scattered about the desktop. Crowell had been working for an hour or more trying to understand the latest from the lawyers. Mushimo's wealth had come from several different enterprises, the largest being a shipping company that imported and exported, dealing with many of the colonies.

All the companies were sold or closed down several years earlier and the proceeds invested in a variety of other ways. He had been relieved to find them all legal. Crowell had known his old master was very wealthy, but the more he delved into the details, the more amazed he became. Mushimo could have been one of the most influential people in the empire, had he chosen to wield that power.

A sudden prickling raised the hair on the nape of his neck. He whirled around just in time to grab the wrists of a black-clad figure. A knife blade shimmered in the light as they tested each other's strength. Crowell was at a disadvantage having to bear the weight of the assassin as he pressed downward.

A surprised look came into the assassin's eyes. His mouth opened silently beneath the mask. He jerked forward, grunting in pain, then collapsed onto his intended victim. Crowell let the body slip to the floor. Akiro stood facing him, watching in satisfaction. He looked at Crowell.

"I swore I would never be too far away again," he said quietly. Then he turned away. "I think it is time, Mushimo."

"What do you mean by that?" Crowell asked.

"Nothing," Akiro muttered.

"That night something else began happening. I started having what I thought were hallucinations. You know, people following me, watching me. Such things as that. I decided the situation was making me paranoid.

"I didn't tell anyone, but I was sure Akiro at least suspected something. I would catch him watching me. He never said anything. Then one night . . . You know, sometimes I still find it hard to believe."

"Someone spoke to you from within yourself," Iroshi said softly. She leaned forward, watching him intently, thinking all the while: how foolish not to have guessed.

"Exactly. How did you know?"

"It happened to me on Rune-Nevas. Who was it?"

"Mushimo."

"Mushimo? I thought it was to be Fotey."

Of course he would choose Crowell. Until now she had assumed that he knew nothing of the companions. Why had Ensi and Mushimo not told her everything?

"Ensi! When I am alone we will talk."

Yes, Laicy.

"It would seem they have kept information from both of us," Crowell said. "I didn't know that you have a companion.

"I also did not know that you and Iroshi were the same person. I did know, after Mushimo came to me, that Fotey had joined with Akiro. That had been arranged before Mushimo . . . uh . . . died."

"Mushimo told Akiro beforehand?"

"Yeah. He was prepared for it."

"He was the only one," she said.

They sat silently for several minutes, digesting the new information. Then Crowell resumed his story.

"Anyway, there were two more assassination attempts in the two years it took to get the inheritance completely settled in the courts. We moved slowly, carefully. We were fortunate that Ozawa was not on the Council at that time. If he had been, he probably would have passed some law to help his claim.

"We've been at loggerheads ever since. With Mushimo's wealth, I'm too powerful for Ozawa to get the better of me.

The same applies to him. His efforts have become more covert mostly through his position, with few direct attacks. I'm sure he thought being on the Council would work more in his favor than it has."

"Have you never tried to attack him?"

"No. Mushimo never found an opening. And he was more familiar with the organization, his sons, how things are done here . . ."

"But you have a whole different perspective."

"True, but . . ."

The door opened, admitting a lovely Japanese woman Iroshi had not met before. She bowed to Iroshi, then to Crowell.

"Robert, it is late. Your guest may be tired and wish to retire."

She moved to his side. Crowell put an arm around her shoulders.

"Lai . . . uh . . . Iroshi. This is my wife, Yumiko."

Yumiko bowed again. Swallowing hard, Iroshi bowed in turn.

"Pleased to meet you, Yumiko."

Crowell's eyes met hers. He also had not told everything. She looked away hastily.

"Yes. I am beginning to feel very tired. I will see you in the morning, I suppose."

"Would you care for some refreshment in your room?" Yumiko asked. "Some tea, perhaps."

"No. Thank you."

Somehow she made it back to her room. Too much! she wanted to shout. She had not allowed herself any conscious expectations of the reunion with Crowell. She acknowledged now the underlying hope that they would have at least the *possibility* of reestablishing their former closeness. That unexpected loss, along with the other surprises, was too much.

"Ensi."

Yes.

"Your keeping these secrets from me makes me most unhappy." The words seemed too inadequate.

Laicy . . .

"Don't interrupt. This is the worst possible time for these secrets to be revealed. I am so angry . . . I don't think I can concentrate on the mission. How could you do such a thing? It has put me completely off balance."

Laicy, calm yourself.

"Calm myself? I am about ready to chuck the whole damn mess. I trusted you and Mushimo all these years. Now, I am not sure I can any longer."

Laicy, we are sorry. We misjudged your reaction and your attachment to Crowell.

"You knew we were lovers!"

Yes, we did. You never told us how deeply you cared for him or that you still did.

"But you are a part of me. You had to know."

I have never probed your memories, your private life, other than when we first met. I knew you were fond of Crowell. But your devotion to the Glaive, as you nurtured it into power, seemed to be your major concern. Then, there was your relationship with Mitchell.

She didn't want to think about Mitchell. Must she now add the crime of using him to her list?

"What about Mushimo's joining with Crowell?"

His joining with Mushimo was done as an emergency measure. After that first assassination attempt, the others and Mushimo decided he needed the extra edge without delay. There is nothing of the Glaive in their joining. Before he knew who Iroshi is, he was not altogether sure of the motives of the Glaive. Mushimo reassured him without too much emphasis. He will be more supportive now, I think.

"If he gets over the revelations of tonight. He probably feels even more betrayed than I do."

During this exchange, Iroshi had paced the room in her agitation. Now she undressed, crawled into bed. The mattress on the floor. Sixteen years came and went in a rush.

"What never ceases to amaze me, Ensi, is how easily I believe you."

Your instincts are good. Never forget, I depend on you, I need you, and would never knowingly jeopardize our relationship. I never act foolishly.

"But . . . I wonder sometimes if what we are doing matters that much. Or if our course is the right one. The more I see, the more I wonder what gives us the right or the desire to make such decisions."

Someone must assume at least a modicum of control. You know that. You see how far-flung the empire is.

Empire! The government cannot even decide to call it by that name, or any name, officially. It is clear the Council members don't know what they are trying to govern; and they spend so much of their time bickering amongst themselves. They accomplish very little.

"Except perhaps the move to Rune-Nevas."

Yes. They are smart enough at least to recognize the usefulness of the Glaive in securing their own positions. That may be thanks to Ozawa. It is a shame that we never got inside the Council.

"We agreed that the danger would come from more powerful groups."

With dangerous consequences. It seemed impossible that they would ever be strong enough or cooperate among themselves enough to be a threat.

"Now we must correct our mistake. I only hope we are not too late."

Ensi withdrew, leaving her to her confused thoughts and emotions. Crowell, married. She felt betrayed, hurt, knowing she had no right to either of those emotions. He had not betrayed her. She was the one who had left. She had not kept in contact. But was the Glaive, and all it stood for, worth the price? Up to now she had paid the toll willingly, blindly. But leaving Crowell had been one thing. Losing him completely was quite another.

She tried to settle in for sleep. Tomorrow would begin the first trial for the Glaive. But tonight she was nineteen again. So many memories. . . .

13

Secret Partner

Behrenstein picked at his food carelessly. He had invited Iroshi to dinner, and she had accepted only because he was a power within the government and could prove useful. He came to the restaurant alone, which had, to all accounts, become his habit since returning from Rune-Nevas. The young lover who had accompanied him at the ceremony must have been discarded.

"Surely the school is not the only thing that brings you this far." He took a sip of wine and smiled sweetly.

"It was a good excuse to visit Earth again," Iroshi replied smoothly. "However, if plans for the school work out, we intend to establish a second headquarters for the Glaive here. On Rune-Nevas we are so far from everything."

"Not if the Council decides to move there." He watched closely for her reaction.

"Is that a real possibility? I mean, there have been so many rumors, but I never believed them."

"According to what I have been told, Rune-Nevas is a definite possibility. One of three, in fact. Argo and Limnos are the other two."

She remembered hearing Argo mentioned as a possibility. It was the headquarters for Ritter Mining, the most powerful of the corporations. Limnos was the base for the Limnos family. They rivaled even Ritter Mining in power.

"It seems to me that the Council would be better off staying here on Earth. If it comes within reach of either of those spheres, it could be taken over so easily."

"Then would you not want to push the selection of Rune-Nevas?"

"No, I would not. I meant it when I said it should remain here. The Glaive is not a political organization, except where politics affects us directly."

They have arrived, Ensi said.

"How do you stand on their move?" she asked Behrenstein, studying his face intently.

"I have no opinion and, of course, no say."

"But you do have influence?"

"Of a sort. I know a few people . . ."

His face went white. He placed his hands on the tabletop as if to stand.

They have just entered the dining room.

"I thought so from his reaction," she replied silently.

Iroshi had purposely taken the chair that put her back to the door, so that Behrenstein was the first to see them. His gaze passed over her left shoulder, locked on the entrance. His face remained ashen, his lower jaw slack with horrified surprise.

They are moving toward the table.

The stricken man started to his feet.

"Don't get up, Mr. Behrenstein. We have not yet finished our dinner."

She turned as two figures approached the table.

"Well, hello, Lucas. Imagine meeting you here."

The warrior/truth-sayer bowed in greeting. Beside him stood a very frightened boy, about ten years old.

"Oh, this is the lad you spoke of."

She smiled reassuringly at the boy, whose eyes did not leave Behrenstein.

"Yes, Iroshi. This is Ivan Tamaroff."

Lucas patted him on the head. The boy looked up adoringly, but fear returned to his eyes when he looked again at Behrenstein.

"He is a candidate for membership in the Glaive," Iroshi explained to her companion. "Lucas found him on Io. So close to Earth. I have not gotten his full history as yet, but I will."

Behrenstein looked at her then. His sickened fear beat at her. Both she and Ensi raised a barrier against it. Still she felt ill.

"Time to make an exit," she told Lucas through Ensi.

"We wanted to let you know we had arrived. I will leave you now." Lucas bowed.

"Thank you, Lucas. Sheera is with you?" Lucas nodded. "I will see you back at the hotel, then."

She turned back to Behrenstein as man and boy walked away.

"An interesting story, I understand," she said. "I have only gotten a small part of it, as I said, but he is a twin."

Beads of sweat glistened on his upper lip. He was so still she wasn't sure his eyes blinked.

"Is he all right, Ensi?" She sipped her tea.

He hears you. His mind is in quite a turmoil at the moment. He will be all right once you give him a way out.

"Getting back to our previous conversation," she said. "It would be better for the Glaive, and I believe the whole of humankind, if the Council remained here. Earth is centrally located among the colonies and not as likely to come under the direct influence of any specific group. Besides, New York is so beautiful."

She waved her cup at the wall of solid glass. Nighttime New York was beautiful with its millions of jeweled lights and the squalor hidden in the darkness.

"As the home world of our species, we believe it should retain as much importance as possible. We would appreciate any help we get in convincing the Council to stay here."

She looked at the timepiece set into the wide gold bracelet.

"Oh, dear, look at the time. I must get back to the hotel. There is always so much work to do."

She patted his hand resting on the table and stood up.

"Give me a call in a few days. We will be here at least

until the end of the week. By then this question of the Council will be resolved, I believe. Good night."

Men turned to watch as she made her way through the dining room. Some knew who she was, some probably did not; either way, she was attractive and different with her natural brown hair and opaque gown. The current evening fashion of hair dyed to match that of a sheer gown did not appeal to her personally and seemed most inappropriate for someone in her position.

The air car was brought to the door, and she was soon at the hotel. Once in her room, she breathed a sigh of relief and made ready to hear the whole story from Lucas. Only the barest details had been available, relayed to her by Ensi as she was on the way to the restaurant. That had not given them an opportunity to elaborately stage the boy's appearance, but there was no time to waste either. From Behrenstein's reaction, Lucas had been correct about the seriousness of the story, and the impact on the commissioner could not have been greater.

Lucas entered the sitting room from one of the bedrooms as she took off the black satin evening cape. The white gown was seductive. She was seductive as she sat on the sofa. It came naturally to her, and she was only vaguely aware of the expression on his face. It was when he sighed, as if remembering the good old days, that she settled into a more modest pose.

"How is the boy?"

"Well," Lucas answered, "he's sleeping now."

He went to the bar and fixed himself a drink and her a glass of wine.

"Does he confirm the story?"

"Some of it. Right now he's too scared to say much. We don't want to probe deeply until I have gained his complete confidence."

He brought the glasses to the sofa, handed the wine to her, and sat at the opposite end.

"I doubt that he knows the whole story. Janue will probe

lightly while he sleeps," he said, referring to his own companion. "I gave him a slight sedative, so he won't know a thing about it."

"All right. Give me the details as you've discovered them so far."

"It was Sheera who first got wind of it. Just before I arrived on Amber to pick up her and Thomas. She got word from someone in the temple that this guy named Larson who was working on the station had once worked for Behrenstein. Apparently he knew more than Behrenstein thought, or else he wouldn't have been let go like he was. Larson had no idea what it all meant. But it was enough for Sheera and me to make a little extra stop on the way here."

"Was there any trouble on Io?"

"No. Everything was handled casually there. Behrenstein didn't make a big deal about the boy or the arrangements there. Security was loose. There was nowhere for the boy to go and no one worried about someone coming in. We got the impression that his lovers have often been kept there. Sheera simply told those in charge that she was the boy's sister. There was a bit of flak about getting permission and all, but Sheera carried it through.

"She did a great job, especially considering that I couldn't be of much help to her."

Iroshi nodded. It must have been difficult for Lucas to leave it all to the young woman. But a truth-sayer could not participate in such a ruse without the risk of being asked a direct question.

"What information did you find, besides the boy?"

"Some medical records were in the files. The doctor who performed the operations was still there, although he wasn't much help. We couldn't probe deeply, since we wanted to get in and out fast.

"A few warriors and their companions were alerted to other possibilities we came across, and a few reports have come in. No one except Behrenstein knows the whole truth.

But enough people know parts of it that we can piece together much of the story as we find them."

"Or at least make him think we can. We don't have a lot of time to go hunting." She paused thoughtfully. "Are we reasonably certain that the surgery was not medically necessary?"

"As sure as we can be. His reaction in the restaurant sort of put the seal on that."

"Tell me everything you have so far, from the beginning."

"Behrenstein has apparently believed, for much of his life, that he was supposed to be twins. Not just a twin, but both a boy and a girl. You see"—Lucas leaned forward intently—"his twin sister is a part of him.

"About two years ago, he decided that he no longer wanted to be a homosexual. He blamed that part of his nature on the domination of the girl twin."

"What made him decide to make the change?"

"No one knows yet. At least not for sure. The opinion seems to be that he got bored."

"Bored?"

"Yes. Boredom, or at least the avoidance of it, seems to have been the ruling force of his life. We'll never be completely sure without a probe."

"Not yet. He has a certain amount of sensitivity and might detect a probe. Or at least become suspicious."

"We're still worried about that, even after tonight? Ivan in our custody gives us the upper hand."

"That is true. We have shown our hand. Giving him another example of the strength of the Glaive might not be unwise. The commissioner was definitely shaken at the sight of the boy. Anyway, go on with the story."

"When he made this decision two years ago, he began a search for twin boys with the proper genetic background for transplanting. The search took about a year. His agents found Ivan and Yuri on a distant, out-of-the-way colony, can't remember the name offhand, and bought them from their parents."

Iroshi wrinkled her nose in disgust.

"They were taken to Io, and as soon as all the tests were made, Yuri was dissected. They used as many of his organs as possible, transferring them to the commissioner. Heart, liver, kidneys, testes, pituitary . . . everything that might have some bearing on his sexual appetites, except the brain. This was just after his visit to Rune-Nevas.

"Ivan was kept around in case any of the organs failed."

Iroshi shivered. It was difficult to keep in mind that Behrenstein was, at the moment, more valuable to her and the Glaive alive than dead. Destroying him would be very satisfying. But his position as Commissioner of Guilds put him in high standing with the Council. His cooperation wouldn't guarantee a favorable vote, but it was a strong step in the right direction.

"Working with someone like him goes against everything I feel is right, Ensi."

This is understandable. Just think of him as a tool which has its uses and which will one day be discarded.

"Have you scanned for him?"

Surface scans only, as we agreed. He is within range. I found him to be the kind of person who will do almost anything to survive. A threat to him, such as this, will not drive him to suicide, thus wasting our efforts. He may make a move against us or the boy.

I would suggest moving the boy as quickly as possible. To some safe place. To Crowell, perhaps.

"No. We have brought enough conflict to Crowell, I think. I won't add Behrenstein to his enemies if I can avoid it."

Somewhere else, then. But not Rune-Nevas. Not until we understand what effect all this has had on him.

"He trusts Lucas. I will let him make arrangements."

She opened her eyes. Lucas sat with his closed, communing with Janue, but he too looked about in a moment.

"Janue has finished," he said. "Ivan knows what happened to his brother and who did it. He does not know why, nor why he was not released. Janue simply found the knowledge and retreated without most of the details."

"Good enough for now. Arrange for Ivan to be taken somewhere safe. Don't tell me where it is unless I ask."

Lucas nodded.

"I guess that is all we can do tonight. Tomorrow I want to work on neutralizing Ozawa, Mushimo's son. He will vote against whatever he thinks we want because of our friendship with Crowell, if for no other reason."

Laicy, wake up.

She snapped awake. "What is it, Ensi?"

Someone is trying to scan you. Raise your barrier so that I can lower mine and see who it is.

She did as he said, waiting calmly for his return.

It is Behrenstein.

"I never guessed that he has that much ability."

He uses a booster with a hookup similar to that of a navigator.

"How does he hide . . . Never mind. We must decide how to handle him."

What do you have in mind?

"I am not sure yet. Does he know that we are blocking him?"

No. He thinks he is simply having trouble getting through. He is not very adept.

"How much longer will keep trying?"

All night, if necessary.

"We have time, then."

For what?

"To decide if this is the time we show him another aspect of the power of the Glaive."

I think that is appropriate.

"Can you . . ."

Yes. I can take care of it.

Slowly Ensi slipped past her barrier. Iroshi drifted into a

meditative state, then lowered her barrier altogether. She saw his display of the twins being taken from their parents. It stopped. Ensi released a burst of energy toward the shadowy presence of Behrenstein. She felt the booster burn out. She heard a scream.

14

Maneuvers

The gallery filled with spectators all talking in low voices. The council chamber below was empty except for uniformed pages and a few aides rushing in and out on mysterious errands. A huge table shaped like a horseshoe and made of dark wood, highly polished, dominated the scene. Sixteen chairs sat empty, awaiting their respective councilors.

The clock on the wall above the table chimed once. All talking ceased, and scurriers stopped exactly where they were. Sixteen councilors filed into the room, and everyone in the gallery stood with a great rustling of elaborate dresses and fancy suits.

Iroshi stood out among them in her Glaive uniform. Her own uniforms were designed exactly like those of the members: cossack-style tunic with sash belt over slender pants tucked into ankle-length boots. The standard uniform was deep grey, not quite black, decorated only with the Glaive insignia on one side of the high collar and one denoting rank on the other side. The membership was so small in number, the only ranking was by length of service. Some day a greater diversity of rank would be needed.

The outfit was completed by a matching color short jacket or cape, the wearer's choice, with deep violet lining. Simplicity was the key, even to the small hat with a tiny feather. The wearer also chose the color of the feather.

The only luxury she allowed herself as head of the Glaive was a variety of colors for the linings and several styles of boots. However, for this occasion, her first official appearance on Earth, she had chosen to wear the standard uniform with matching cape. The feather in her cap matched the violet of the lining. The ever-present katana and wakizashi were thrust under the sash. Glaive members were among a small number of people allowed to wear their weapons within the chamber, which included heads of the guilds.

Everyone, councilors and spectators, took their seats. More attention was given her than the councilors and their proceedings. Not many Glaive members had ever visited Earth, and her being its leader added to the interest. Everyone wanted a glimpse of Iroshi. She heard her name whispered several times as it rippled through the crowd.

She turned her attention to the councilors.

Ozawa is second from the right.

"Scan the others first and see where they stand. Gently, Ensi, but we must know the votes thus far. Leave Ozawa until last. Then see how deep his feelings are against us."

The councilors discussed some minor application from a lesser planet. The mining company entrenched there wanted to expand its operations into previously excluded territory. The excluded territory held some importance to several of the families living on that world, but their petition could not hold out against the strength of the mining company.

Such decisions were made in public meeting once a week just for the show. Admittance to these performances was much sought after and difficult to obtain. Behrenstein had made arrangements at Iroshi's request.

The proceedings droned on, and she feigned interest in every word while waiting impatiently for Ensi's findings. At the distance, her own sensitivity was useless; she couldn't direct her attention as narrowly as Ensi could. The show was elaborately staged but the outcome certain from the beginning. The company would get its way because there was no one with power who chose to contest it.

She studied the men and women selected to wield power

in the interests of the empire. Each councilor was in the pocket of a powerful family or corporation in service to their own interests, each hoping to hold onto at least the semblance of power. Ozawa was the only one not in league with another power broker and was most likely the instigator of the plan to move the Council. The obvious selling point was greater independence and, since no one pulled his strings, he could convince by example.

Fifteen people would take Ensi some time to probe. Iroshi continued her study of the councilors, ranging in age from about fifty to over a hundred, she guessed. They looked like none of them had smiled in years, and then only in the line of duty.

Ozawa was the most comfortable in the scene. He clearly feared little.

She took particular notice of the man near the center of the table. One of the younger councilors, she sensed from him an attitude of cynical amusement, even across the distance. He did not belong with the others and was probably not accepted by them. Through the miniature binoculars she saw his nameplate on the table in front of him: Gherrold Roberts. He might be worth getting to know.

He might be. He is the only one completely in favor of leaving the government headquartered here. A few of the others are shaky. They seem nearly equally divided about where to move.

"Identify them so you can find them later. I want you, Mushimo and Janue to scan as much as possible. We need to know which ones will be the easiest to bring over to our side."

Very well. Do you want me to probe Ozawa now?

She hesitated. She sensed from him the same kind of danger she once saw in an old man in her travels. Alerting him to her abilities, even though they were shared with Ensi, might put him too much on guard. Just looking at him, though, she guessed that he seldom relaxed. The possibility always existed that he might be prodded into acting indiscreetly if she pushed a little.

"Do it, Ensi. Maybe it is time to move a little more boldly."

Iroshi kept her gaze casual as she continued watching the proceedings. Depending on how sensitive he was, Ozawa could be made aware of her interest if she watched him too closely. But it was she who found his gaze glued to her. One eyebrow raised as their eyes met.

"He knows," she thought.

She bowed her head and smiled. He nodded in turn, but the stony expression did not change. Their eyes maintained contact for mere seconds, but the intensity made it seem much longer. Ozawa was the first to look away, lending a semblance of attention to the day's business.

Sorry, Laicy. He is very sensitive.

"It's all right. That may have been a step in the right direction by forcing some action. What did you find out?"

The proceedings ground on through three more petitions while Ensi recounted what he had learned. Ozawa knew of her association with Crowell, putting her on the other side of the feud. He was unhappy at her presence on Earth but not surprised, further confirming their suspicion that it was he who had tried to prevent or delay her arrival. Ozawa felt he had several reasons to oppose her. Not only was she in league with his great enemy, but she was also attempting to block the move of the government.

He wants to depose you as head of the Glaive and become its leader. Possibly by incorporating it into his present organization. He realizes the possibilities of the Glaive. That is as far as he has gotten in formulating a plan.

Ensi went on to explain that realization of the potential inherent in the Glaive was the basis for Ozawa's determination, and suggestion to the Council, of making Rune-Nevas the new headquarters. He was of the opinion that Iroshi did not fully appreciate what she controlled since she had not yet made use of its potential. At least, not until now. He suspected her desire to influence the Council, and the reasons behind that desire, meaning that he might have underestimated her. A mistake not likely to be repeated.

He will stop at nothing to achieve his aims. He is the most ruthless man I have ever come in contact with.

"Perhaps that is also his greatest weakness."

She stood with the others in the gallery as the councilors filed out, their business for the day concluded.

Everyone milled around the room aimlessly, meeting, talking, being seen. They served no tea at this reception, so Iroshi merely carried the drink she was offered. She located Ozawa in the center of the room and approached him. He looked up as she neared; again their eyes locked.

"I have been wanting to meet you, Mr. Mushimo," she said eagerly. "I have heard so much about you." They shook hands.

"And I you," he returned. "Everyone knows of Iroshi of the Guild of the Glaive. Few have met her."

They exchanged a few formal pleasantries, watching each other like fencers looking for an opening.

"I understand you are here to open a school for members of your Glaive."

"Oh, no," she corrected. "We intend to use your father's old dojo to train new members. Robert Crowell was my first teacher; then I spent two years with Mushimo. It seems like an ideal arrangement if we can come to terms."

"Yes. I understand Crowell is an excellent teacher."

Their attention was diverted by an aide who came up to her.

"Excuse me, Iroshi, but Mr. Garson would like to meet you."

He spoke her name like a title. Most people not introduced to her did the same.

"Of course, I would be delighted." She turned to Ozawa. "Please excuse me."

They shook hands again and she moved away with the aide.

She stayed at the reception a long while, meeting all the councilors and many other officials and dignitaries. After the first encounter with Ozawa, she completely ignored his presence, giving the impression that he was of no more or less significance than anyone else in the room. With the exception, that is, of Gherrold Roberts, with whom she talked a good while.

Roberts was the only councilor who seemed to realize that the Council and the government it represented was too weakened by time and circumstance to maintain its integrity. Its presence on Earth, the birthplace of their species, was its one remaining source of strength, and the main reason anyone paid any attention to it at all. That and the planet's being at the center of the populated galaxy.

Nothing could be gained through association with any other organization, and, in fact, the opposite would occur. Soon, he stated, the Council would exist in name only.

The arguments spilled out once the young man was assured that she thought as he did. In spite of his strong feelings, he was cynical enough to believe that his arguments would fall on "deaf ears and petrified minds." He felt that the move would be made and, once done, he would resign. Until then he intended to observe his prophecy come true.

Iroshi listened, and encouraged him to remain on the Council no matter what happened. Ensi reported on Ozawa's movements around the room. He never let her get long out of sight. She felt it when her attention wavered from Roberts and Ensi reported it.

"He has not tried a probe of any kind?"

No. He is sensitive but has no apparent ability to reach out to anyone with his mind. No doubt he employs people who can. We must be on guard continuously.

"As we always are."

True. But even more so now. This man is utterly ruthless.

Leaving Roberts in order to mingle a bit more, she did

not need Ensi to tell her of Ozawa's attention. His interest was intense, nearly palpable. It washed through her consciousness in a continuous wave, tugging at her to pay attention. She managed to maintain her distance both physically and emotionally. However, the intensity was such that at last she raised the barrier, leaving Ensi outside of it to collect data.

Before long it was time to leave. She had decided beforehand to be one of the first to go, thereby avoiding the impression that she and the Glaive were in any way dependent on the Council. Everyone in attendance was as eager to say goodbye as they had been to say hello, not glad that she was leaving, but to have her attention, as if she truly knew them.

They were impressed, Ensi said once they were in the air car. *Some votes have been swayed by your presence. At least two might easily turn from Rune-Nevas for the new headquarters.*

"That makes seven possibles. Still not a majority. All we need are two more ready to vote that way. It would seem that the Glaive's reputation is standing us in good stead."

Do not discount your own reputation. You are a beautiful woman, glowing with power. You would have made a remarkable queen.

"Why, Ensi. Sweet words from you?"

Such banter often caught him off guard, although his sense of humor had improved during the past years.

I caught that from someone at the reception.

She smiled at his defense, then changed the subject.

"Will you be able to find the councilors later tonight?"

Yes. I have their expected locations and thought patterns. A few will be too far for contact. Mushimo, Janue and I will find what we need.

It still worries me that Ozawa has been alerted.

He paused as if choosing his next words carefully.

Mushimo's son could present us with the first instance requiring complete subordination.

"No, Ensi. We must avoid that at all cost. Killing him would be less abhorrent than taking over his mind."

Never exclude any path, Laicy. The stakes are too high.

That evening Iroshi and Lucas were enjoying an after-dinner conversation in the sitting room. While she was away, he had sent Ivan away, in Sheera's care, to some hiding place, returning to the hotel shortly after her. Ensi and Janue were about their task with long-distance help from Mushimo.

Iroshi broke off in the middle of a sentence. She sat still with a look of total concentration. Lucas remained quiet, watchful.

"Ozawa is here," she said after a moment.

"I felt a presence," Lucas commented. "He's strong."

Iroshi nodded.

"Don't let him know you are here. Hide in the bedroom and listen." She paused again. "He is trying to sense us. Block him."

Lucas nodded and retired to his room.

A knock came, and she uncurled from the sofa to admit Ozawa.

"Good evening, Iroshi." He bowed.

"Mr. Mushimo, what a pleasant surprise. Won't you come in?"

She stepped aside, motioning to the center of the room.

"Thank you."

He stepped across the threshold.

"Please, call me Ozawa."

"Of course. Have a seat. May I get you something to drink?"

"No, thank you." He sat at one end of the sofa.

"What may I do for you?"

She lowered the barrier. "Ensi."

I am here, he replied instantly.

"I wanted to talk to you about Rune-Nevas. I understand that you do not want the Council on your planet."

"That is true."

"My wish is to try to convince you that such a move could benefit the Glaive as well as myself."

Something is very wrong, Laicy. There is another presence. Like nothing I've felt before.

She started to expand her consciousness, so full of Ozawa's presence, searching.

No! Pull in. Whatever it is, there is great danger.

"Actually there is nothing to discuss, Ozawa. I am quite sure of what is best for the Glaive."

"Let me just leave this report for you to read." He handed her a communication disc. "Perhaps we can discuss it later."

"I will be glad to look it over. Let me give you a call in a few days."

"I ask for no more." He stood. "Thank you for seeing me."

She let him out. Lucas reappeared, his puzzled expression matching her feelings.

"What was that all about?" he asked.

"He was pinpointing us. There was another presence. I think we can expect some kind of assault very soon."

But, Laicy, Janue and I should be with you and Lucas just in case, Ensi argued.

"The barrier will be up and you will continue the search. You have the key if it is necessary to break through.

"You will know if I am in trouble," she insisted. "We need that information quickly if we are going to get the votes we want."

Ensi agreed reluctantly.

It was just after one o'clock in the morning when her screams woke Lucas.

15

The Maze

The old nightmare. Falling through darkness, then the iciness of water in deep shadow. Struggle to get out of the pool. Slow steps in search of a way out.

It had been a very long time since she had visited that place, but those feelings were all well remembered. Familiarity did not diminish the impact. She struggled to waken but was locked in the dream cycle. Fear, like she had not known in many years, wound its way through her mind. Something else was there. Its presence like fear itself, surrounding her.

She screamed as tendrils pinioned her. Malice strengthened its grip. It surrounded her with malice. It *was* malice. It fed on the fear that poured from her in torrents.

Paralyzed, she watched as the black shadow built something in the distance, even as it continued to hold onto her. Piece by piece the something grew, immense in size, with walls three times her own height.

It had no right. This was her dream, her mind. She struggled against the bonds. They only drew tighter.

The work ceased. The pieces all fit together like some giant puzzle. Malice lifted her into the air, over its creation, showed it to her from above. A maze, black on black. The creature hovered on silent wings, then dropped her carelessly, and she sprawled in the central block.

Stunned, she lay still for several minutes. She pushed to a sitting position, movement bringing realization that she was no longer bound. A new danger stalked her. It sought her now, sniffing in corners, how near she could not tell. She scrambled to her feet. There must be a way out.

In the dark she ran into walls, fell over hidden snares. Each time she stopped, the sounds of pursuit grew louder. Bruised and weak, she raced on. Backtracking when the path became a dead end. Pausing at each corner in fear of coming face to face with the pursuers whose snarls sent chills up and down her spine.

There! The exit. A grey section within the black. She ran. It was closing. Run faster! Getting smaller. Oh, god.

She crashed into the wall just as the moving section closed against the other side. She struggled to her feet, jumped for the upper edge. She slid down the smooth surface, fingers just short of the mark.

Leaning against the wall, she fought to regain her breath and listen. Something pushed her back a step. The wall was moving. She put her back to it. Three more walls closed in toward her, forming a box. A second scream tore from her throat.

Once more she was immobilized. The four walls pressed against her. Darkness was absolute. Breathing hurt as her own arms pressed into her sides. Malice lifted the box, held it suspended, then dropped it into nothing. She grew dizzy, then sick, turning end over end. A person could die this way.

With a jolt, the box stopped falling and hung in the air again. With all her strength and determination she braced against the walls with feet and hands. All four panels exploded outward. Iroshi held her breath, waited to fall. An instant passed. She opened her eyes, found herself suspended in black nothing. Waiting.

Wind cooled her sweating body. Cool became chill. She shivered. Shiver turned to tremble to convulsive spasms. The wind swelled into a gale. Her body twisted and turned. Then she was falling again.

Darkness paled, grew lighter, brighter. She dropped onto a hard surface of pure, blinding white. Malice glared white, burning into her eyes. A sound in the distance tugged at her. She should focus on that. It was important. Malice didn't like that.

The white surface disappeared from under her. She slipped, fell, slid down a slanting floor, still blindingly white. Far below a black maw opened, black against white. Edged with white points. The maw clicked shut, teeth meshing. She slid downward, slowly, inexorably.

In the distance the sound demanded attention again. She tried to concentrate. Into the maw she slid, sharp teeth ripping at her back. Her eyes glazed over with a red film. A soft wet mass pressed, curling her, forcing her to tuck her head between her elbows to keep from suffocating. She wanted to cry, but there was not enough air.

Between gasps she heard the sound, nearer and insistent. It had meaning.

"Ensi," she screamed.

Fons Ensi Fae Goron.

She heard! The words that lowered the barrier.

"Ensi!"

She screamed his name again. She felt him rush in past the barrier. Janue was with him. They struggled with a form, too far away for her to see clearly. But she could see, and that meant that she was free.

Mushimo rushed to her side, comforting and concerned. It was the first time she had seen him. He had been only a voice inside her head for so long. She clung to him as she clung to sanity. The struggle with malice continued, and she buried her face against Mushimo's shoulder. She did not want to see its face.

The first scream brought Lucas straight out of bed. He rushed through the sitting room into Iroshi's bedroom. As he went, he lowered the barrier, allowing Janue to return.

Ensi cannot get through to her.

Lucas palmed the light control panel. Iroshi lay rigid,

covers thrown back. Her body glistened with sweat. He took hold of her shoulders and shook her.

"Iroshi!"

She cannot hear you. We think something has invaded her mind.

"How can we help her?"

We must get her attention. Watch over her.

"Can anyone else help? Mushimo or any of the others?"

They are all alerted. Mushimo is with us.

He was gone. Lucas had a moment to feel the loneliness of being without Janue. It was as if a part of him was gone, unlike the times when the barrier was up or Janue communed with one of the others. He was truly gone, had joined Ensi in what they could only hope would not be a vain attempt at lowering Iroshi's barrier.

All that passed in a moment. He got towels to dry her skin, then covered her nakedness. He pulled a chair up to the bed and sat watching. When she screamed and thrashed about, he held her, protecting her from herself.

Late in the morning, Crowell appeared. Mushimo had told him of Iroshi's danger, and he had left immediately for New York. During the three-hour trip he remembered over and over the practice in the dojo on Siebeling and the aftermath. How much he had enjoyed making love to her. Too bad he had not remembered earlier how much he cared for her.

Crowell's arrival gave Lucas his first opportunity to grab some food and take a shower. He hurried just in case he was needed.

Early in the afternoon she began shaking. Her skin was icy and damp again. The two men dried her with fresh towels Lucas had ordered from room service. They piled every blanket in the three bedrooms on top of her. Still she shook until the headboard rattled.

They held her down as she thrashed about once more and stood helplessly as she gasped for air. Whenever she was quiet enough, they dried her off.

She screamed Ensi's name, and they looked at one another, hoping it was a good sign. She screamed the name a second time. A moment later she clung to Crowell, who was closest, crying as if her world had ended.

Lucas sat in great relief, watching, feeling only a little jealous, as the crisis seemed to have passed. He walked to the window and turned off the screen. The sun was setting, clothing the world below in darkness, a world of people and things that knew nothing of their struggle. Above, a few stars, unconquered by the city lights, blinked softly, pretending to care.

Mushimo talked as Iroshi cried. His words shattered against her refusal to admit them. He persisted, battering against her defenses, wading through the turmoil. At last she heard.

Laicy, we cannot rid you of this malice. We can hold it, but only you can force it out. You must do it now.

"I cannot."

She trembled, wanting to push him away because he asked too much of her, instead clinging to him for support.

You must.

"I don't know how," she wailed.

But you do. You know the power of your mind. The sword is not your only strength. Concentrate. Gather your power back in. Thrust your fear aside. See its face.

"No."

See it, Laicy. Face it. See its hideous face. Know it. Know that you are stronger. Recognize its weaknesses. It has no mind of its own. It expands on your worst memories. That's its only power. It sees the fear in you and uses that.

She raised her head. Malice looked directly at her, drooling as fear gripped her heart at the sight of it. It was small, yet power emanated from the lustrous black surface. There was no intelligence lighting the orange eyes, only hatred and lust.

Use your memories, your emotions, to grasp it. Expel

malice like a stray thought which never belonged. Look at it, Laicy. Already it suffers from your recovery.

It howled when her gaze did not falter. Newfound hatred reinforced her determination to make her stand straight, away from Mushimo. Malice was terrifying, but she gave herself over to rage. The eyes of the enemy glowed, returning hatred, getting brighter as its victim no longer accepted her own impotence.

Mushimo continued speaking encouraging words. Words she had heard from him before, and which had meaning. They conjured up youthful power and great happiness. Ensi and Janue released malice as Mushimo nodded.

It leapt for Iroshi, crashing into her barrier as she had crashed into its walls. She shattered the barrier herself, letting the pieces crash downward onto its prone form. She thrust her will at it, forcing it backward. It moved, fighting with every step. It struggled savagely at the edge, trying desperately to stay within her mind. She pushed, overjoyed at the realization that she was indeed stronger.

She followed it out as it raced for shelter, seeking solace and protection. It tried to shake free of her, then to keep her out. She pressed as it returned to itself. She assaulted it there, seeing no fear in it, only confusion. It had never failed before at the only thing it knew how to do. For malice, the blame must rest with someone or something else.

Iroshi moved back slightly as it thrashed about, seeking a victim for its rage. Distanced a little, she could see that the creature's being was filled with memories of earlier victims both human and nonhuman. Their remembered terror filled niches, filed away with gruesome care.

She groped past the niches, seeking a weakness with her own irresistible thoughts of vengeance, and saw . . . Ozawa. He and the creature. Master and servant. They had bonded many years before. She drew its attention to the man, pushed it toward him. Ozawa stared at her in disbelief.

"Your creature comes for you," she told him with satisfaction.

He was even more off guard than she had been. With no time to anticipate or react, he was immediately overcome. It enveloped him in dark shadows. She withdrew, unable to watch and unwilling to help.

It was after midnight when Iroshi opened her eyes. Crowell slept in the chair beside her, and Lucas sat on the other side of the bed. Lucas smiled, but she did not respond.

"How do you feel?" he asked.

"Could I have some water?"

Her voice was weak, but a most pleasant sound to him. As he went to the table for the water, Crowell stirred, then came fully awake to see that she was back with them.

She slept for another day and a half, waking intermittently to find one of the three people watching over her. She was surprised the first time she found Sheera there. Later they told her that the young warrior returned from her errand for Lucas as soon as she learned of Iroshi's danger. The boy Ivan was safely on his way to a hiding place.

She said little except to ask for some food. It arrived in the room service chute just after she emerged from a long shower, wearing a cozy robe and her hair turbaned in a towel. She ate leisurely, not because the food was good, but because the simple, everyday act provided an anchor within her own reality. After it was all eaten, she took her time over a cup of tea, hesitant about joining her friends in the sitting room.

The time could not be put off forever. She dressed slowly, weak from the ordeal, took time with her hair, then walked into the room. Crowell watched a newscast on the vidscreen. Sheera lounged in a chair, staring into space. Lucas had his eyes closed, in the attitude of meditation. They all looked up as she sat on the sofa, and tried not to stare at her as she hesitated to begin.

The fear came again that they might be disappointed in her. Iroshi was not indestructible, had been nearly eaten alive by a little black creature and its master. The first test had been passed, but not without being close to fatal. More than likely they expected greater strength from their leader. Especially Sheera, who was so young, so new.

You must tell them what happened.

She cringed slightly at Ensi's voice inside her head.

"Sorry, Ensi.

"You are right, of course. They have a right, a need, to know in case they are similarly attacked. Talking about it will help me. Won't it? Or will it make it more real?"

It will help. All of you. They will not ask. It is up to you to begin.

"Why won't they ask?"

They respect you too much.

"Still? After this?"

Yes. They understand no one is indestructible. They never expected you to be. Even without all the details. They know what happened from the companions, but what it means can only come from you.

For a moment she considered his words. Understanding and appreciating his words, and the sentiment behind them, gave her a little courage. Might as well get it over with.

Aloud she said, "Would anyone like a cup of tea? There is some left in the pot."

"No, thanks," said Crowell.

Sheera and Lucas accepted, and she got the pot from the bedroom and poured. They settled down, all three prepared to switch from waiting to listening.

She began slowly, telling them about the old dream and its origin.

"The creature used that against me, to set me up for what it created in my mind. Ensi and Mushimo say it is not bound by normal rules. They describe it as a mind vampire. Where it came from or what it actually is we have no way of knowing. Not yet."

"How did it get in?" Crowell asked. "Mushimo said that your barrier was up and Ensi was outside of it."

"I have no idea. Neither does Ensi. We have discussed the possibilities, but the only way of being sure is to go back inside it."

She shivered.

"Like a cat burglar, it has its secrets. I believe it is possible that it could slip between the elements of energy which make up the barrier, perhaps mix in with them." She shrugged. "I don't know."

Iroshi went on to tell the whole incident in minute detail, including her own reactions. She told it in a dispassionate voice, struggling to keep her face blank. Her eyes betrayed her several times when tears appeared in the corners. She stopped for a moment to catch her breath.

"I left them there," she continued. "Locked together, possibly for the rest of their lives. The creature will feed off Ozawa's mind as long as it lasts. He is a strong man with great willpower, but without help, like I had, he will never be able to break free. He may live a very long time."

She stopped talking, stared at nothing. Telling it had shaken her almost as badly as the experience itself.

"Why didn't it get through your barrier the second time?" Sheera asked.

Iroshi looked at her questioningly, not understanding what she meant.

"When you attacked it, it came at you but crashed against the barrier."

"Oh." Iroshi thought a moment.

"Possibly because I was ready for it. I wasn't asleep. Or maybe it was not really trying. I mean, it was reacting instead of acting. It didn't take time to insinuate itself. It simply lost control, became enraged.

"One thing we must do is learn from this experience. As much as we can. What happened to me directly is one lesson. What happens to Ozawa is a second. The third would be to make direct contact with the creature, but I see no way that can be accomplished safely.

"There may be more of the things out there somewhere,

or another creature with comparable abilities. We must have a defense, an automatic one so that we will not be taken by surprise as I was. And as Ozawa was, in the end."

Crowell looked over at her, his expression solemn.

"We got word a while ago that they found Ozawa, raving out of his mind. He was taken away for observation. No one has any idea what's wrong with him."

"Except us," Iroshi whispered.

16

The Battle

The mattress on the floor had been exchanged for a standard bed with mold-mattress, which would conform to her shape. Its height made it easier for Iroshi to get.in and out of bed. She insisted on undressing herself, and Yumiko, who had put herself in charge of the invalid, shooed everyone out.

"When you are settled in the bed, call to me. I will be just outside."

Iroshi nodded, but there was nothing Crowell's wife could do for her. However, as she crawled under the cover, feeling even weaker, she called out.

"All right."

Yumiko entered, followed by one of the serving women carrying a pot of tea.

"Tell Crowell I need to see him," Iroshi said sharply.

Both women looked at Iroshi warily; then their features flowed into a soft look of understanding. Obviously she was still quite ill and was impatient because of that. They bowed and left the room.

"Stupid women," Iroshi muttered. "Stupid custom, bowing."

She broke into tears as her own words recalled her first awkward bow to Mushimo. Her feelings dwindled from sorrow to self-pity. Her thoughts moved to what had become a recurring theme.

"I should never have allowed them to talk me into heading the Glaive. It is too great a responsibility. More than I can handle. More than any one person should be expected to handle."

Sobs shook her thin body. A knock came, but she did not hear. Nor did she hear the door open. Crowell entered the room, sat on the edge of the bed, and lifted her in his arms to embrace her. She cried on his shoulder, grateful for his warmth and strength. She clung desperately. It seemed like such a long time since someone had held her close. Since anyone had loved her.

Love! This man was married to someone else. He didn't love her. She pushed away.

"Why is your wife still here?" she demanded. "Didn't we agree that all those who are not qualified warriors were to be sent away until we are sure it is safe?"

Crowell was taken aback by the sudden change but recovered his equilibrium quickly. For several days her moods had been utterly unpredictable, although this bitter tone was a new twist.

"Yumiko is a qualified warrior," he explained reasonably. "She also wanted to stay so that she could help you in any way you require."

"I require nothing except to be obeyed!"

"Laicy," he began, his teeth slightly clenched, "I love you still. I will do almost anything I can to help you through this. But I am not of the Glaive. Even if I were, I would not be ordered about in this way."

Rage distorted her features and left her speechless. No one talked to her like that. Her eyes searched for her katana.

She was too weak to sustain the anger, and it burned itself out. His words and tone were too formal, and looking into his eyes she saw the pain she had given him. She sagged farther into the pillow, all emotion draining from her, leaving her hollow and spent. He bent down and kissed her forehead.

"Sleep, my Laicy. Everything is settled for the night. No attack will come yet."

He squeezed her hand.

"Rêst and regain your strength, for we will need it. Your strength and your wisdom."

He brushed her forehead with his lips and left. Her hollowness became filled with sorrow and self-doubt. Tears flowed down her cheeks. That one night of horror and hatred had robbed her of her strength and determination. So far, nothing had helped her to regain them. Something else had been lost, but she didn't know what to call it. Perhaps it had no name. Perhaps it was only the glue that held everything else together. When that was lost, a person truly fell apart. Just as she was doing.

No, she had worked too hard, cared too much, to lose it all now because of some hideous little monster. Anger sprang forward, anger at the beast, its master, herself, at those surrounding her and caring for her.

She cried until she felt utterly spent. She lay quietly with swollen eyes closed. Peace, she cried out silently. Then Rune-Nevas appeared. The old scenes of her world when it was young and belonged to others. The beautiful panorama, full of promise and desire. Ensi was playing with her mind, something he had not done since the early days. She didn't mind. The scenes and his feelings for his home soothed her now as they had long ago.

"Thank you," she whispered.

"You're absolutely sure that Toshiro plans to attack?"

Crowell asked the question even though he knew the answer. Behrenstein would not look at him directly. The commissioner was a man afraid, caught between two powerful forces, either of which could easily destroy him. He knew that. He also knew that neither the Glaive nor Toshiro would allow him to maintain neutrality.

He nodded. "Yes. Although there are stockpiles of arms within the fortress, they had collected a few things from outside. They are also gathering air cars of various sizes."

The fortress was screened, and the companions had stopped scanning when the ninja locked themselves inside. Toshiro was outside from the beginning. His hatred for them, and his desire for revenge, were so strong that his feelings penetrated the screen. Iroshi felt them through her own pain and lethargy. Her wounded spirit absorbed them, held them, until she gave in to the tensions. Even in her sleep she tossed and turned, restiveness stealing her hopes of peace. According to Ensi's periodic reports, she was at the moment locked into that restless sleep.

After telling them about the experience with the mind vampire, Iroshi had withdrawn into herself. The others were surprised, since she had seemed so strong, recovering physically from the ordeal. Sitting around the New York hotel room, they were unsure of what to do. A second in command had never been named. Someone had to take charge. Lucas and Sheera deferred to Crowell. His companion was Mushimo, Iroshi's teacher, and his teacher as well. With his greater knowledge of the enemy and the territory, and with Ensi's help, Crowell was the logical choice.

As soon as word came of Toshiro's plan to attack, Crowell decided they should move back to his compound. The decision was discussed with Iroshi in one of her more lucid moments. She offered a few suggestions, including informing Mitchell, through the companions, to be on the alert for a possible attack on Rune-Nevas. Several warriors assigned to worlds closest to the base world were ordered to return to their headquarters. The rest were summoned to Earth for the coming battle. Some had already arrived, but it was impossible to tell if there would be enough to successfully defend against Toshiro.

During the flurry of activity, the original purpose for the visit to Earth was not forgotten. In addition to keeping an eye out for Toshiro's activities, Behrenstein was ordered to keep his finger on the pulse of the Council. Removing

Ozawa would have simplified their efforts, and might have been accomplished, were it not for his brother's continued presence. Toshiro's organization was still powerful, and the councilors were making no decisions until the final outcome was decided between the two forces.

"If only Iroshi could make an appearance before them," the commissioner said. "Will the business take much longer?"

Crowell was brought back to the present by the question. Glaive business was the explanation for her seclusion.

"A great deal of curiosity has been generated by her absence," Behrenstein continued. "In spite of the explanations, everyone is guessing as to the real reason she has not been seen. Some say the prospect of meeting the ninja forces frightens her."

"Is that all that is said?" Crowell asked coldly.

"No. There is a very strong rumor that she is ill—near to death, some believe."

Crowell looked quickly to Lucas, who sat silently. Had Behrenstein formed that as a question directed at the truthsayer, the near accuracy of the rumor might have been confirmed.

"She is simply occupied by business, as we have said, and is preparing for the coming battle," Crowell said. "Thank you, Mr. Behrenstein, for your help."

The commissioner recognized the dismissal. He turned away to wander through the garden toward his own quarters.

Crowell looked straight overhead at the sunny blue sky, ignoring the silence as it lengthened. Lucas and Sheera held their own council. Everything had been said a hundred times. The plan, such as was possible, had been made. They had only to await the arrival of as many warriors as could make it before everything exploded. They could only hope that their numbers would be sufficient.

"Excuse me, Crowell." He jerked upright at the interruption.

"Yes, Akiro," he said a little too sharply. For an instant he thought more warriors must have arrived.

"There is a man at the gate who says he is Laicy's father. He wants to see her or Lucas."

Crowell looked at Lucas, then Sheera.

"Iroshi didn't tell you?" Lucas asked. Crowell shook his head.

"I'll go and talk to him," the warrior said.

Lucas walked off with Akiro. Behind him Sheera was telling the story of finding Jonathan Campbell.

Although he was outwardly calm, Campbell's narrowed eyes revealed the tension he felt.

"What's going on, Lucas?" His voice had only a slight edge to it. "I'm hearing all kinds of rumors about Laicy. When I get *here* I see all kinds of security. Is she okay? Can I see her?"

Lucas nodded to Akiro, then slowly escorted Campbell along the walk toward the garden. As he recounted only the barest facts about Iroshi's condition, Janue scanned the older man. He then conferred with Ensi on the advisability of allowing father to see daughter under the present circumstances.

Lucas, he is no threat. Ensi says it may help to let him see his daughter.

"Let me introduce you to our host," Lucas said as they approached the table. "Then we'll see if Iroshi is awake so that you can see her."

Sheera stopped talking. Lucas could see by Crowell's expression that he had heard enough for his suspicions to be aroused.

"Robert Crowell, this is Jonathan Campbell, Laicy's father."

The two men shook hands, sizing each other up. Crowell

knew Campbell only as the father who had abandoned his family back on Siebeling, and quite recently had been part of a plot against Laicy. On the plus side, he had saved his daughter's life on Amber.

"So you're Crowell," Campbell said. "Laicy told me about how you taught her kendo."

"She was my best student." He turned to the young woman who approached and bowed.

"Would you please take Mr. Campbell to see his daughter? She's expecting you," he said, turning back. "We can talk later."

Campbell nodded his thanks and moved after the woman. As they watched him go, Janue began his report. Mushimo and Lorin picked it up to relay to Crowell and Sheera.

After landing here, Campbell made a discreet inquiry in an effort to discover who hired him to sabotage Laicy's trip. He discovered the man's identity at nearly the same time that man discovered Campbell's presence on Earth. It was Toshiro, who did everything he could to find out why the job was not completed.

No one was particularly surprised by those facts.

Campbell was forced into hiding, instinctively knowing that it would not be wise to let Toshiro know he was Iroshi's father. He has had several adventures and near escapes in the past week. It took some time for the rumors to reach him that she was in trouble or ill. He also learned that Toshiro planned an assault on her and her friends. As soon as he found out she was here, he came to offer his help in the coming fight. Or anything else where he might be useful.

"Are you sure he can be trusted?" Crowell asked.

Yes, he is sincere in his concern for his daughter.

"He's a good fighter," Lucas added. "At least he was effective on Amber."

"I know," Crowell answered. He did not yet look convinced.

• • •

The guards around the perimeter were alert and determined, a mixture of the earliest Glaive warriors to arrive and some of the more advanced students of the dojo, along with a few crewmen from the racers. In two weeks, just better than half of the available warriors had come. The rest were on the way but would not arrive in time, although Toshiro waited an unexpectedly long time to attack. At last report the odds were running approximately 125 to 40 against them, which may have given the ninja leader the idea he need not hurry.

Crowell shook his head sadly. Walking the perimeter at two in the morning was not conducive to optimism. This was not the first night he had found sleep impossible, leaving their bed to Yumiko. She had been awake last night and tonight, he knew, but he remained silent as he slipped into his clothes, then went out into the night. She knew his pain because she loved him, had been his wife for eleven years.

He loved her dearly, but without the passion he had known with Laicy. That passion had been rekindled when his former pupil stepped back into his life just days ago. Days? How quickly a life could change. Anger had beaten down that passion, made it impotent with feelings of betrayal, and worse, of being forgotten for so many years.

The struggle between passion and battered feelings continued until word came that Laicy was in deadly peril. Without regard for his own feelings or Yumiko's, he rushed to her. Concern won out for a time, passion tempered with deep love and renewed respect.

The dream woman still lay in peril, battling for her own survival, alone beyond anyone's help. The real woman silently watched the man she loved struggle with his own emotions and expectations. Right and wrong had no bearing here. Fairness was relative to what each wanted to ultimately take away from this scenario.

Crowell shook his head. The same thoughts over and

over, rolling around in circles. No beginning, no end. Too
many conflicts at one time. He could empathize with
Iroshi's struggle. So many things had occurred recently
to upset her life. There was no stability and no place to
hide.

They come, Mushimo reminded him quietly.

They had known Toshiro's forces were near for the past
two hours. He blinked, saw something move in the surrounding light moat inside the fence. A black figure
crouched in a small natural shadow, nearly invisible. Crowell moved in his silent way toward the warrior posted just
ahead. He was of the Glaive, and when Crowell touched the
man's shoulder he nodded.

"Is everyone alert?" Crowell asked Mushimo.

Yes. They are all awake and prepared.

"How many have come?"

One hundred forty-eight. Toshiro is with them.

"So it all ends here, tonight."

We can only hope.

"And Laicy?"

*She is aware. Her agitation increases. We must let her
find her own path in this.*

How incongruous it all was, Crowell thought, that a full
battle was to begin momentarily. The future direction of
humankind could very well be decided this night. Not with
high-tech weapons or high-flown ideals, but with very old
and revered swords, spears and knives, wielded by two
groups believing in ancient traditions.

"Is everyone set?" he asked again as tension mounted.

Yes.

"Now we wait once more."

Not long.

Warriors poised for battle in early morning darkness.
The ninja would have to cross the brightly lit field, coming
out of darkness and then back into darkness, which should
prove disorienting.

As defenders, they had the advantage of choosing the

ground on which to fight. The presence of the companions gave an added edge: the ability to fight in the dark. Superior numbers was the advantage of the attackers, along with their perverse loyalty to their leader. They knew that Toshiro had made glowing promises of the rewards to be given after conquest of the Glaive. He had never lied to them before.

They will attack any moment. Toshiro will send them in waves instead of all at once.

"Any surprises yet?"

No. Only their number, which is no real surprise. Weapons are as expected. But they see well in the dark.

A wail rose; it began. The exact direction was impossible to pinpoint and did not matter. The effect was more important as Crowell watched more black figures move through the light toward the darkened complex. Did they know warriors watched? That they were ready to meet them? That did not matter either as the first clang of sword meeting sword rang through the air. Then everyone knew. Shouts rose as ninja met warrior all around, black-clad attackers outnumbering the defenders three to two.

Crowell, defend!

He spun, blocked the descending sword. He had sensed a presence at the moment Mushimo barked the warning. The dark form of the ninja was barely discernible to his eyes. The companion directed the sword when the host was unable to detect the next cut. The sounds of battle were everywhere. Scattered cries of pain punctuated contact between and among warriors.

Crowell ducked as a blade whistled through the air from behind. He came up, bringing his sword with him. It connected, disemboweling the adversary from crotch to chest. His blade continued its arc overhead, catching the first ninja on the right shoulder, cutting downward. The dying body fell backward, nearly pulling the sword from Crowell's hands.

Exhilaration coursed through him. It had been a very long time since his skills had been tested in this way.

Lucas fought on the side of the complex almost directly opposite Crowell. A dying ninja lay on the ground close by as a second one stepped into view with a spear. The longer weapon gave him the ability to maintain distance from the sword but, even though he used it very well, it could not match the speed of the shorter blade. Lucas took him even more quickly than the first.

Sheera is besieged, Janue informed him.

With Janue's guidance, the seasoned warrior made his way to the younger woman's side. Three ninja were taking Sheera's skills to the very limit. Lucas separated one of the three from the uneven match.

The ninja turned into the new adversary, hindered neither by the darkness nor lack of ability. His sword lashed out. Lucas, caught off balance for an instant, felt the razor edge catch his upper right arm. No pain registered, only the tickle of blood running down his arm.

Finish him, Lucas. Sheera is once again one against three.

"I'm trying!"

Somehow, just as on Amber, they seemed to know that Sheera was younger, less experienced. Lucas pushed the ninja's sword left, traced a half circle in the air, to slice downward. The ninja had started to move backward, so that the cut went through the skull, dividing his face into nearly equal halves. The result was no less deadly than a fully met cut, although the body had not crumpled to the ground when Lucas whirled back toward Sheera.

The younger warrior had killed one of her adversaries, but she favored her left side, where blood stained her shirt. Lucas came between Sheera and the two assailants just as one swung a deadly arc. Swords rang. Lucas pushed the man away.

Sheera is down.

Lucas stepped over her body and stood astride her. He fought off the two like a demon, determined they would not give the young warrior further harm. He wounded one on the left shoulder, but the man was able to get away. The other ran untouched, disappearing into the darkness, probably in search of an easier target.

Another wave of them comes.

It took a moment to catch his breath. Grabbing both of her arms, Lucas dragged Sheera toward the door of the building behind him. The woman moaned once; then she was taken by one of the servants who had volunteered to stay behind. Lucas returned to his position, seeking the next adversary.

Akiro was deep into the void. Two of the enemy lay dead, and one was severely wounded. Fotey did not speak, merely guided Akiro's focus as needed. His sword cut the air silently, sounding only on impact. His arms and legs positioned themselves easily, without thought. The ninja before him was the best swordsman he had faced so far. They had been fighting for quite some time. Akiro blocked a downward cut. Stepping to the right and turning slightly, he executed a perfect horizontal cut. The ninja was cut in two just below the waist.

A fresh ninja, from the third wave, approached. He had seen his predecessor go down, having watched most of the fight. Now he moved forward, as if he had an idea of how to beat the old man. At the first ring of their swords meeting, the sky seemed to lighten perceptibly. The moon would be up soon to reveal the carnage in an icy glow; sunrise would not be long behind.

The ninja grew angry as his strategy failed to pierce Akiro's defenses. The approaching dawn seemed to remind him of his failure.

Laicy!

Fotey called out unexpectedly. Akiro lost concentration, leaving an opening. A scream tore through the air. The sound, so full of anguish and rage, brought a momentary halt to all action. For several heartbeats no sound was heard, no weapon dealt death. Then a warrior's kiai, a scream of more human proportions, stimulated the action to resume.

She joins the battle.

17

To Fight

A single shout went up from the scattered Glaive warriors when word came from the companions. Iroshi was well enough to fight with them. She was there, her voice identifiable among all the voices raised in battle cry. They were given new hope. They fought with renewed vigor. The attackers fought warily, wondering at the cause for the sudden strange behavior.

The reason for her sudden appearance on the scene was not broadcast, nor did it matter to the warriors. The agitation she had suffered had increased unbearably for several days as she sensed the nearness of attack. The sounds of battle coming through the walls roused her, nearly driving her over the edge into madness as she lay there afraid to act. Watching her, Yumiko had considered tying her to the bed.

Just as the eastern sky lightened with the first silver arm of the moon, Iroshi leapt from the bed. Yumiko rushed toward her, but stopped when she saw the look on Iroshi's face. Iroshi the mad, the warrior, would not tolerate interference.

Hurriedly, she threw on her pants and tunic, tied them with the sash. She thrust her wakizashi through the sash and grabbed her katana from the rack, drawing it from its sheath. The blade reflected death on its mirrored surface. She stared at it for a long moment, wondering whose death. Then came a crippling pain as she felt a sword blade pierce the body of her father.

With an inhuman cry she raised the sword overhead,

186

holding it with both hands. Yumiko gasped at the exaggerated look of madness in her eyes.

Iroshi stalked across the room, slammed the door aside, and stepped out onto the veranda. With her normal kiai she raced into the fight. The first encounter brought on the red haze; everyone moved slowly. Their weapons hesitated, giving her time to react before they could come close to her. Several ninja backed away as she began the skillful slaughter of their comrades. No one could stand up to her onslaught. She passed into the void. Her sword and spirit drank in the blood of the enemy, fed on the fear. She was the earth on which the bodies lay as life departed.

Suddenly it was over. There were no more ninja to maim or kill. Those who had not fallen fled as they either saw or heard of the insatiable woman warrior. Iroshi was loose, dealing death in an unimaginably thorough manner.

Iroshi stood encircled by her followers. Even they were afraid, not understanding what they saw, unsure that they even wanted to understand. She stood there, breathing hard, sword poised for combat. The morning breeze dried the blood on its surface, shielding the steel from the sun's rays as it slid its full bulk above the horizon.

Birds did not greet the dawn. They waited to see if the day would find peace or further slaughter in first light. Nothing moved in that field of death. A wounded warrior moaned softly. That was the only sound as Iroshi stood, seeing for the first time.

A shudder convulsed her body. She blinked, relaxed her stance, lowered the blade. Crowell moved to stand before her. Gently he took the sword, handed it and his own to the nearest warrior. She focused on him.

"Crowell?"

He nodded.

"It is over," she said weakly.

"Everything?"

"Yes. I am free, healed."

She swayed slightly. Crowell steadied her. Lucas took

hold of the other arm, and the two of them led her back to her room.

Smiles broke out on every living face. Iroshi said she was healed, and Ensi spread the word that it was true.

Late in the afternoon the bodies were cremated on several large pyres: eighty-five ninja, fifteen warriors, one student. The scene recalled the mass cremation in another courtyard a millennia before.

Doctors treated the wounded bedded in the complex until recovery was complete. Those who were unhurt or who suffered minor wounds helped with the cleanup until exhaustion caught them up. Iroshi went back to her bed for several hours, after a good hot bath.

Just before dusk she joined Crowell, Lucas and Akiro in the garden. Smoke from the pyre still rose into the air, turned red by the setting sun. The sweet, meaty smell of blood had nearly been cleansed away. She had just visited Sheera in her room. She and all the other wounded would recover, barring any unforeseen complications, with one possible exception. Jonathan Campbell's wounds were serious enough that the doctors could not be very reassuring. She mourned deeply the deaths of those she had known in the Glaive and Crowell's young student. Later she might mourn the deaths of the enemy.

She sat between Crowell and Lucas. The three men gave her a long look, smiling in relief at her recovery. She smiled back self-consciously and poured herself some tea.

"Well, what has been happening since this morning?"

Crowell, still unofficially acknowledged as second in command, spoke.

"Toshiro led the flight back to the fortress. From there he took off in a racer, leaving most of his ninja behind. Several of them committed suicide, apparently an old custom Toshiro revived when he reestablished the cult."

"That seems out of place in this day," Iroshi commented.

"Any more than a battle fought with swords?" Lucas asked.

"I suppose not," she admitted.

"The Council voted unanimously to remain on Earth," Crowell continued. "They voted not long after word reached them of the outcome here."

The following silence became uneasy again. They had been at ease with one another over the years, had been able to speak their minds easily. The possibility of losing that familiarity forever weighed heavily on her mind. There were many questions to be answered, she knew, but they could not bring themselves to ask. Once more. Were events outpacing their abilities to absorb, to go on from that point in the old way?

She wished they would ask. Answering would be easier than just beginning out of thin air and would reassure her that their relationships had not changed.

"It is like in the hotel."

I know. They await your lead.

"Have I lost their friendship?"

In a way. They loved you before you became Iroshi. They still do, but you have changed. Not only personally, but ... You were, respectively, student and ronin to them before. Now you head your own guild. They have seen you do things, experience things, be things, they never even conceived possible.

"Like today."

Yes.

"I do not want to be isolated like that. Not from them."

It is lonely, I know ...

"No, you don't know. Not anymore. It happened to you so long ago that the feelings have become distorted by time."

Ensi fell silent, withdrew. At first she was angry at his reaction. Then the realization grew that she had been unnecessarily hurtful. He had once said he and the other spirits no longer felt emotions. Even if that were entirely true, the memory of past emotions need not be blunted. Perhaps their impact was even greater if the emotions themselves were truly lost, experienced now only through the host, shared but not possessed.

"I am sorry, Ensi. I should know better than to make such all-encompassing judgments."

No one knows everything or practices everything they know.

She looked at each of the three men thoughtfully for a moment. Their faces, their mannerisms, their voices were so familiar. She loved them in so many ways. That must be the first thing said.

"You are my closest friends," she began. "With the exception of Mitchell and Ensi, you are my only friends. Our relationship goes beyond what we have within the Glaive."

They all nodded. Akiro and Crowell wiped at their eyes, as if that was one of the things they needed to hear.

"Now, about what happened this morning." She paused. The whole incident had not yet been examined or even thought about except to acknowledge it had happened. She really had no idea what she was about to say, except that it would be the truth.

She reminded them of the days of intense agitation because she knew, on her own, when the attack was coming. What they did not know was that she had such a fear that she would not, could not, take her place among the warriors. After the invasion of her mind, there was very little of which she was not afraid.

"Ensi had not said a word to me all night. I lay there in the bed as the ninja were sneaking toward the compound, coming over the wall. I knew they were there. I grew even more afraid.

"Sounds of the fighting came to me. The clash of steel, the cries of the wounded. And I was a coward, keeping to my bed.

"Suddenly, I became so angry. At myself for being afraid. At Ozawa and Toshiro for forcing this fight on us. At the creature which tried to take my mind. At the ninja who wounded my father. I felt his pain and I screamed; I held the katana over my head as if . . . as if swearing vengeance. Yumiko was there at the time."

She looked at Crowell. He looked surprised. His wife had said nothing about it. But then, they had only spoken to each other when he was bathing sometime after the battle.

"I vaguely remember rushing from the room, onto the veranda, then into the fight. At that time nothing I did or saw was real to me. I entered the void almost at once. My actions were dictated by necessity and the . . . the souls within the sword. For the first time they directed me, moved me.

"As I fought, all the fear, hate and anger went out through me, through the katana, into . . . the bodies of the enemies as I struck them. Fighting, killing, wounding was a catharsis draining me of all those bitter emotions."

Tears appeared in her eyes, and she blinked them back. Her breathing became slightly rapid.

"When it was all over, and I stood there, surrounded by all of you, I felt clear for the first time in days. The feeling of violation had been purged."

She fell silent, considering whether to go on or how to say the rest. She had worked hard building a reputation for ruthlessness, and this would not fit that image. She cleared her throat, took a sip of tea. Her friends sat, waiting for the rest of it.

"It took violence . . . killing, bloodshed . . . to rid me of my own pain. What kind of person am I who can kill so easily for her own benefit? What kind of organization will the Glaive become if I continue as its leader?"

"That wasn't the only reason you were fighting," Crowell said.

"What else? In defense of my life? I was in no immediate danger. The rest of you were handling the attack well without me."

"Hell, Laicy!" Lucas exploded. "We were just holding our own. When the next wave of ninja came, we would have lost several more warriors. Your sudden appearance scared them enough to stop that next wave. If fighting to protect yourself isn't sufficient, how about fighting to save your friends?"

"We were close to exhaustion," Crowell confirmed. "Lucas is right. Your intervention saved us. It saved the Glaive. In the end, it saved the Council from making a very serious mistake."

"Those of us who are members are very serious about the Glaive and its purpose," Lucas continued. "We believe we can make a difference in the future of our race. That means the Glaive as a whole must survive, and its leader must survive, honorably. As a group we are important, and possibly the only chance."

"Don't forget, Laicy." Akiro spoke for the first time. "It was the wounding of your father which finally drove you to act. The selfishness you see in saving yourself is one of the traits which help people survive. Very few can claim to be entirely unselfish. But someone who can blend the two into pertinent action should never be ashamed. You acted with honor."

After another pointed silence, someone turned the conversation to more general subjects, including some of the future results of the Glaive's victory. It had probably become the most powerful organization in existence. The trick would be to retain that power while slipping back into the behind-the-scenes role. That would take some time.

For the second time that day, exhaustion muddled their minds. After a few surreptitious yawns of her own, Iroshi excused herself. She went to say good night to her father, found him asleep, then went to her own room. Wearily, she undressed and slipped into bed.

She had never been so tired. In the short time since she had left Rune-Nevas, a whole lifetime had passed. It was impossible for so much to happen in just a few weeks and survive intact. But, she had survived.

Mulling over what she should do next, she delayed sleep.

She needed to be alone for a while, to think about it all. To talk about it with Ensi some, but mostly to herself.

Suddenly it struck her. She needed Mitchell, his rock-solid view of the universe and its inhabitants. She wanted the earthiness of his lovemaking. For the first time she wanted his love, the love always offered, never accepted. She must go home.

That decision helped her relax, and she was soon asleep. For a couple of hours she forgot everything, lost in the peaceful depths of sleep. It was still dark when someone shook her shoulder.

"Iroshi, wake up." It was Yumiko. Iroshi sat up groggily.

"What is it?"

"Your father. He wants to see you."

"Is he all right?" Hastily she threw back the blanket and began to dress.

Yumiko stopped her frantic movements, held Iroshi's hands.

"He's dying," she said softly. "I am so sorry."

A lump rose in Iroshi's throat, nearly choking her. She resumed her frantic efforts to get dressed.

"No, it's not fair."

She rushed out, still buttoning her tunic.

He was awake when she got to his bedside. She sat down beside him and took his hand while sniffing back tears, trying to see his face. He squeezed her hand.

"Sorry, kid. I wanted to spend more time with you."

"You are not going anywhere. Not yet."

"Pretty soon. I know it and so do the doctors." He stopped to catch his breath.

"Are you in pain?"

"Naw. They've taken care of that."

"I did not realize . . . I didn't want to believe you were so badly hurt."

"I didn't want them to tell you before. You had enough to think about. It's almost done now, and I wanted you close. I'm not afraid. Only wish I could be around to see all the great things you and the Glaive will do."

He drifted into drug-induced sleep.

"Ensi."

We are trying, Laicy.

Her right leg, supporting her as she sat on the edge of the bed, went to sleep and her shoulders ached a little, but she didn't shift positions for fear of waking him. He moaned once or twice, but his expression was clear. She watched over him, overwhelmed by the feeling of loss. This on top of everything else. Was it all her fault? Her mind conjured up the question but was too numb to search for the answer.

Her stomach felt bottomless. Tears stung her eyes, backing up to create a headache behind her green eyes. A nearly overpowering desire to scream worked in her throat. A need to be held as she cried tugged at her heart. Was something good supposed to come out of all this?

Laicy. There is nothing we can do for him except make it as easy as possible.

"Why?"

He has never meditated, at least not on the level necessary. There is not enough time to teach him to draw inward sufficiently to make the transition. He was not frightened by us . . .

"Us?"

Mushimo was with me. We explained to him who we are, what we do, and why we were with him. He recognized that there just is not enough time to accomplish it. Even though we started immediately after he was wounded. We knew it would probably prove fatal.

"When he said 'they' had taken care of the pain, he meant you and Mushimo, didn't he?"

Yes. We did that and explained about the Glaive and its goals. He meant it when he said his one desire was to see the ultimate outcome. Otherwise his mind is quiet. He has few regrets, and even those he hasn't dwelt on. He is more at peace with himself than most people at this time.

He awakens.

"Thank you, Ensi."

Campbell opened his eyes slowly, blue eyes looking into green ones. She smiled.

"I am sorry it did not work, Father."

"Oh, I'm not sure I would want to live forever, anyway. I've already seen the universe through unveiled eyes." He squeezed her hand.

"Laicy, don't ever give up what you're doing. It's important. What Ensi called honorable."

His hand relaxed as the blue eyes closed. A few minutes, and he stopped breathing.

Once more smoke rose in the still air. Sunrise added its fire to the scene. Iroshi watched through a mist of tears, knowing nearly everyone was there to pay their respects, but unable to feel their presence. Even Ensi was silent, and she felt very alone.

Someone put an arm around her shoulders. She knew it was Crowell without seeing him. She blessed his silent presence, which he gave until it was over. Then he steered her into the garden and sat her down at the table, where he, Lucas and Akiro joined her.

"What will you do now, Iroshi?" Crowell asked the question uppermost in everyone's mind. "You're welcome to stay here as long as you want."

"I'm going home."

"When do we leave?" Lucas asked. She smiled at him.

"If you don't mind following later, I intend to go alone. I need to be by myself for a while. The trip back should be just long enough."

Lucas nodded his understanding.

"Crowell, if you agree, the plans for a Glaive presence here on Earth will be left in your hands. I still want our young warriors trained here in your dojo. There are now five companions without hosts. They will be matched here."

Crowell nodded. A servant girl brought a pot of tea and a bottle of very rare brandy. She set the tray on the table. Yumiko followed, ready to serve, as the girl bowed and departed. Yumiko lifted the bottle and looked to Iroshi, who nodded. No reason they couldn't indulge now. They were among friends.

As Iroshi took her glass, she looked up into the soft eyes of Crowell's wife.

"Thank you, Yumiko."

A smile lit the brown eyes and she bowed, understanding everything those three words meant between them. She bowed to them all and went back into the house.

Iroshi stood, raised her glass.

"To the fallen."

The three men stood. Four glasses touched.

"The fallen," they echoed.

Any other time, any other place, that would have been very trite.

18

Revay

The darkness of space had no depth. Shining stars were too distant to make any difference. So much blackness could suffocate some people just as if a pillow were put over their heads.

To Captain Ferguson, space was liberation. It was planet-fall that smothered him. Too many people, too much color and fresh air. He glanced over at Thomas on the navigator's couch, all plugged into the ship. He knew. All navigators knew. Ferguson turned back to the bow window, which wrapped around the bridge. The screen was off so that he could look out at his home. In reality, the window was an unnecessary part of the ship. The control bank was alive with instruments, detectors, electronic screens that would tell him everything that was out there, friend or foe. These windows were just not enough for people, who needed to see where they were going, even when there was nowhere to see.

Leaning back in the chair, he let his mind wander. The ship took care of itself, with Thomas's help. Borden, the first officer, was off watch. Liang, engineer, wasn't due on for another hour. Iroshi was in her cabin, where she had stayed most of the past two and a half weeks since they had left Earth. She puzzled him. The Iroshi going back to Rune-Nevas was not the same woman who had left there nearly six months ago. Nor was she the woman who fought the ninja in Crowell's compound.

He had been there during the battle. Most of the racer crews stayed with their ships, gathered at the port, to guard them against possible attack. Knowing, however, that the main attack would be at the compound, a few volunteers left the port and were among those defenders.

Ferguson had fought beside Iroshi on Amber, and he felt an obligation to be with her on Earth too. She burst on the scene almost beside him. Never had he seen anyone fight as she did. Even he could see that she was deep in the void he had heard about. She knew him to be an ally, but he had been sure she did not recognize him.

The memory haunted him, in his dreams and his waking hours. Like now. Every time he closed his eyes, or lost concentration, he saw her, slaughtering like a merciless killing machine. When there were no more enemy bodies to be felled, she stood in the midst of it all looking as if she had been deprived of something she wanted very badly.

Two days later he returned to the racer to prepare it for departure, without seeing Iroshi again. When she arrived at the port two days after that, ready to head home, Ferguson expected the same people to board who had come out from Rune-Nevas. For whatever reason she decided to travel back without the cook, and Sheera was to be left behind until her wounds healed. Iroshi went immediately to her cabin, and had emerged only three times since liftoff.

"Captain."

He whirled around in the chair. Iroshi stood behind him, staring out the window. He took a deep breath, trying to slow his heart.

"Yes, Iroshi."

"There is something out there. Something threatening."

He looked over the console. No lights blinked; the screens were blank.

"The instruments don't detect anything."

"We do."

"We?" he asked.

Her voice was distant, her attitude that of a person in deep concentration.

"I will explain that someday."

She looked at him for the first time.

"There is something or someone out there, Captain. Its presence is shielded from us. I think we had better prepare to defend ourselves."

He nodded and turned to the console. First he summoned Borden and Liang to the bridge. Then he activated the external weapons: two rapid-fire depleted uranium guns and a laser cannon. As he worked he watched Iroshi out of the corner of his eye. For a moment he suspected the danger came from within the racer. Then she looked at him. Her eyes had become calm and clear. They remained that way as she stared out the window. She concentrated, as if by force of will, that the unknown would make itself visible.

"Can you tell how many yet, Ensi?"

Three, maybe four. Perhaps we should try to outrun them.

"No. They are probably as fast as we are. Maybe faster. And that would be postponing the meeting."

Postponing? Why?

"It is Toshiro out there."

You cannot be sure. Even I cannot tell.

"I am sure. Who else could it be? I sense him, the same hatred and need for revenge."

"The detectors are picking up something," Ferguson's voice cut in. He made a few adjustments. "We should have picked them up sooner. They must have some way of absorbing or dispersing the outbound signals."

With a definite direction now, he narrowed the field for each detector.

"Four of them. Borden, see if you can raise them on the comm."

Borden broadcast the standard hailing message. The four ships coasted closer once Ferguson cut the speed of the racer at Iroshi's request.

"Ensi, can you teach me to go into revay?"

Probably. But why?

"I will not let this crew be destroyed because of me. Toshiro pursued me because he wants to destroy me. If I give him what he wants, he may let the racer go. Be ready."

Aloud she said, "Borden, please turn off the comm for a moment. Captain, I have a message for you to send to Toshiro."

"Toshiro?"

"Yes. In one of those ships out there."

"How do you know . . ."

"Do you have a slate and stylus so I can write it out for you?"

Liang turned in her chair to hand Iroshi the slate and stylus. She took them and, moving for the first time since appearing on the bridge, she sat in the empty chair next to the navigator's couch. As she thought over the wording, she glanced at Thomas. There was a frown on his face. Through his link with the racer, he knew something was wrong. His mind maintained contact with every system, and he knew.

She bent over the slate, concentrating on the words. When the message was finished she read it over, made a few minor changes, then carried it to Ferguson. He took it, read a little, stood up and began pacing. He finished reading, approached Iroshi, and handed her the slate.

"No. I won't do this."

"Why not?"

"It's my duty to protect you above all else."

"It is also your duty to obey me."

"I won't let you sacrifice yourself."

"Captain, one of the ships is signaling," Borden said.

"I have no intention of sacrificing myself, Captain. Nor do I intend to let Toshiro escape again."

"Captain?" Borden called urgently.

"Do it, Captain. Now."

Ferguson turned to Borden. "Put it on the speaker."

". . . hail the Glaive ship. Respond or we will commence firing."

"This is Glaive ship 313," Ferguson answered. "Who are you and by what authority do you make such threats."

"By the authority of superior numbers. Who is speaking, please?"

"Captain Ferguson. And you are . . ."

"This is Captain Trair. We believe you have a passenger on board."

"And if we do?"

"We want her."

Ferguson stood silently for a moment. He looked at the words on the slate, then at Iroshi. She smiled and nodded. He let out a long sigh and turned away from her.

"I'm afraid that's impossible."

"You will send her to us, or we will destroy all of you."

"You don't understand. She's ill . . ."

"We don't really care, Captain."

"But . . ."

"You have ten seconds to agree, Captain."

Iroshi stopped listening and turned inward as Ferguson continued to argue.

They believe him.

"Have they dropped the shield?"

Yes. To save power. It takes a great deal of energy to maintain. They only used it to sneak close in. Toshiro is aboard the lead vessel. Are you sure you know what you are doing?

"Yes. Right now I want you to seek out the nearest Glaive presence. We need to let them know where we are. As soon as I am in the capsule, you must lead me into revay. We will attack the navigator, and quickly. We must do all we can to prevent their attacking this ship."

While she had been talking to Ensi, Ferguson had capitulated and worked out the details of the transfer with Captain Trair. The racer ceased accelerating, fired its braking jets. It hung motionless.

"He believes you are only doing this because I am dying, Captain. You played your part well."

They started toward the tube aisle.

"As soon as I am far enough away, I want you to get out of here at top speed. Do whatever you must to save my ship and this crew."

"What about you? How do you plan to . . ."

"Other Glaive racers will be coming this way. Join up with them, but do not be in a hurry to return here."

She held out her hand. Ferguson took it reluctantly.

"I plan to see you again, Captain. Just promise you won't be surprised by anything that happens."

His confused expression deepened. Iroshi grinned.

"You might even hear that I died."

She stepped into the capsule before he could reply. It was shaped like a torpedo, and the only way to occupy it was to lie down. As the cover was sealed, she touched the hilt of her katana. For a moment she peered out of the view plate. The capsule was inserted into the tube; she took a deep breath and closed her eyes. It was uncomfortably confining.

"All right, Ensi. It is time."

May I ask one question first?

"Of course."

Did you know Toshiro would be waiting for us?

"Know? Not exactly. I expected him."

Why did you not tell me?

"I knew you would object to my actions."

Strenuously. But . . .

"There isn't time, Ensi. I must be dead by the time the capsule is taken aboard Toshiro's vessel."

The tube opening closed, and air pressure began to build.

Very well. You remember how you found me that first time. Go deep within yourself. Even deeper than that time. Ask no questions. Say or think nothing at all.

She turned inward, sank within herself. Beginning was easy. She had done this regularly since their first meeting. The way led through memories and experiences. Shadowy figures of friends, acquaintances and enemies greeted her unknowingly. This was different from the void, for it was important to hold onto her own psyche, to keep it separate.

Very important in revay, Ensi broke in quietly. *You must not lose the feeling of what it means to be you. The essence of yourself. Go deeper.*

You are going so deep into yourself that you will come out on the other side.

She saw her birth, felt the pain of leaving the womb to become a person, and her conception. Backward. Everything disappeared, replaced by a darkness, seemingly empty. Panic rose. It was too much like the water chamber.

Quietly, Ensi whispered. *You must pass through this. Deeper. Deeper.*

Bright pinpoints of light appeared. As she watched, they grew larger, getting closer. They whizzed around, coming uncomfortably close. She began recognizing them. There was greed and hatred going past together. On the other side, kindness chased ambition. The lights were the emotions and personality traits held in common by all people. But they were all the same size, as if she was just as evil as she were good. That couldn't be right. Justice chased cruelty to her right. They all appeared and reappeared.

Deeper.

Something was wrong here. She wanted to stay and work it out.

Deeper.

She relinquished the hold and descended. More memories, but none of them her own. Where did they come from? As they formed and disappeared, she realized they were genetic memories. Memories of her race carried from generation to generation within the cells and fluids that came together to make her an individual. Memories of a personal nature, of loving and dying, pleasure and pain.

It began to run together, an overwhelming cornucopia of senses and emotions.

Deeper.

The assault grew less hectic. Individual feelings formed.

Becoming too strong. Overpowering her with their intensity.

Deeper.

Darkness again. Floating. She sensed the end was near. A whirlpool grabbed her, spun her around and around. She fought to keep from being dragged down.

Let go.

Startled, she did as commanded. Faster she spun. Sinking into more darkness. Down. She screamed as she turned inside out.

19

Navigator

Captain Trair looked inside the capsule ruefully. Suddenly, he was pushed aside roughly.

"What is it?" Toshiro demanded. He looked inside, then cursed.

"Confirm that she is dead."

Toshiro moved to the window above the tube opening. Trair motioned for the medical officer to step forward. The doctor checked several pulse points while the scanner verified the diagnosis. Iroshi was dead. He turned to the captain and nodded.

"She's dead, sir," Trair said to Toshiro.

The leader clenched and unclenched both fists at his sides, trying vainly to contain his rage.

"Captain Trair," said a voice over the telecomm. "The Glaive racer is taking off at full speed."

"Kill them!" Toshiro ordered coldly.

"Ensi, help me get into the navigator's circuits."

This way.

She had no eyes or ears or fingers, could only sense his presence, hear his thoughts. She followed without understanding how she did it. There was a sensation of passing into a living mind, then out along a narrow path. A human consciousness stretched along that path, occupied only with reading and guiding the ship of which it was an integral part as long as electrodes remained connected between man and machine.

"Ensi, do you know how the navigating is done?"

No.

"Neither do I."

They sped along the path. Here was her old dream of navigating, being one with the machine that guided ships through time and space. But there was no time to enjoy the sensations. A kind of vision was beginning to develop, and she could see the navigator's presence as if it were a long cord. She and Ensi followed it until, at last, they found the basic consciousness. The man became aware of them at the same moment.

"Keep him busy, Ensi, while I try to figure this out."

She studied circuits and paths, slowly realizing that a navigator's joining with a ship was entirely different from that experienced by Nevan companions and their hosts. Where she and Ensi maintained separate identities, the navigator's mind merged with the ship's artificial intelligence. How completely depended on the personality of the navigator. She understood now why someone like Captain Ferguson would not be content as a navigator forever. It could suck a person up if he or she was not strong, could become the only thing that mattered.

Concerning the problem at hand, she saw several ways of proceeding. Forcing the navigator to do what they wanted would be too time-consuming and perhaps impossible. His own survival depended on the safety of the ship, and vice versa. Probing the mind of the navigator could also take too much time. Trial and error could wreak a lot of havoc, perhaps as much as deliberate action. A combination of tactics might work to best advantage.

"Ensi, probe his mind for what we need. Can you do that and keep him out of my way?"

Yes. What will you do?

"Just start poking around and see what I can figure out on my own."

She had learned a few things from conversations with her father and other navigators. All the descriptions were vague; she had not realized how much so until now. The only certain bit of information was that there was direct access to all the ship's circuits, including its guns.

Circuits piled on circuits. Were these the ones for the guns? One way to find out. She activated them one after the other, sending pulses outward. Something happened, but there was no way to tell exactly what.

Did it matter? For now the most advantageous thing was to confuse the enemy. She sent pulses out on random circuits. With practice, it became easier, and she worked faster. A new sensation worked its way through. Toshiro and his men, unable to locate the cause of the problems, were panicking.

"What the hell . . ." shouted Trair.

One of the cannons had just fired, followed by the second. Explosions pierced the blackness.

The short-range laser cannon activated, striking the nearest racer. A puff of smoke appeared where the beam had pierced a section of the outer hull. That racer's captain telecommed a worried question but was cut off in midcomplaint. The comm officer was unable to reestablish contact.

The computer started the wounded racer into a spin, disrupting the artificial gravity. Live bodies impacted against wall, ceiling and floor, along with a few pieces of loose furniture and equipment on the way.

The laser cannon fired again. Trair leapt for the telecomm control to warn the target racer, the one that had started in pursuit of the Glaive ship. He stopped, hand poised over the controls; the strike flashed in the viewer port.

Iroshi kept impulses moving along circuits. More and more she understood what was happening, where each circuit led. Using other circuits, she saw each action, each weapon fire and the resulting impact or miss, or the movement of the racer. Every action and reaction moved along her own living circuits. The coolness of space felt right along the outer hull.

Feel it. See it. Was this how it became when one was a navigator? As she relaxed, feelings and impressions filled her senses utterly.

A searing jolt brought her back to the more immediate reality. Another of Toshiro's racers had returned fire with its laser. She felt surprise, sensed the surprise of those inside her. There was also a kind of pain from the wound in the hull.

She fired a grenade at the offending ship. A hit! But she was also hit again. Air was escaping.

"Ensi!"

Here.

He was right next to her.

"I can handle this puncture but . . . Is there some way you can get the capsule resealed?"

To protect your body? Yes, I can. One of the ninja will help.

Ensi disappeared. A sealer patched the hole. She resumed the attack.

The frantic crew pushed buttons, toggled switches, palmed sensor pads, everything effectively blocked. She flexed electronic muscles, pulled in her concentration. Two of the other three racers were hit. One was not damaged beyond a hole, now patched, in its hull. The second was more or less disabled, but its crew frantically made repairs. Whether or not their efforts would be entirely successful she could not be sure.

As she turned toward the disabled racer, she noted that the vacuum suits within her own ship were locked in. The telecomm was disabled.

You are safe, Iroshi. What do you intend to do?

"Ram one of the other ships."

To what end? Will you kill them all?

"No. But Toshiro must be destroyed or he will be a constant plague for the Glaive to deal with."

But the others.

"This is no different from the fight at Crowell's. In war, soldiers are killed. Simple fact, Ensi."

I know. I had hoped . . . that it was finished on Earth. You seem to be going about it so coldly.

"Do I?"

She made a note to examine her feelings later. In the meantime, she continued maneuvering the racer.

"The crew in the other vessel will have time to evacuate once they realize what I intend doing. The impact should rupture the hull of this ship. This crew, and Toshiro, will not survive."

The racer picked up speed gradually. She tried to move slowly and deliberately enough to give ample warning to the other crew. But there must be sufficient velocity at the moment of impact to effectively destroy both vessels.

Two figures emerged from the target, drifting ever so slowly in the direction of the third racer. The immobile ship launched a grenade that impacted just above the window on the bridge. Pain distracted her.

Her speed increased. Two more figures separated from the ship. Another grenade crossed the blackness between them. In the ship's present condition, the spring launcher was the only weapon properly aimed at the menace bearing down on it. The grenade hit near the previous impact point, widening the hole in the outer hull and breaching the inner one before repairs could be completed.

A third grenade found its mark at point-blank range. The metal hull of the driving vessel crumpled as it buried its nose into the other. Within the ships, the scream of bending metal vibrated the walls and circuits. A final figure detached itself from the disabled racer. Iroshi hoped that it would get sufficiently clear of the destruction.

She continued the thrust of the engines, completely piercing the hull, impacting against the other engines. Broached, they exploded under the stress. Fire flashed and went out in the airless void.

• • •

Toshiro desperately tried to free his vac suit from the locker. Terrifyingly unsuccessful in his efforts, he looked around for another possibility. The capsule protruded from the tube where someone had pushed it out of the way. There would be air enough in there until he could be picked up.

He tried to pull it from the tube, but it was wedged in and would not budge. He looked around for a wrench or something with which he could force it out. Just then the racers collided, the impact buckling the bulkhead and freeing the capsule. The torpedo shape flew into the chamber, pinning Toshiro against an inner wall. He pushed with all his strength as it slowly crushed the air from his body.

The air inside the ship was sucked out. Crewmen dropped from lack of air, dying before suffering the explosion of blood vessels and lungs in the vacuum. Toshiro slumped over the capsule, his dead eyes peering in at Iroshi's still face.

20

Final Decision

Lucas and Ferguson were the first to board Toshiro's racer. They lumbered around in their vac suits, searching through the debris. Their mutual fear for Iroshi's safety kept them silent.

Vac suits were still locked in the racks. So far they had seen three bodies, none of them near the suits. Nor had they seen Toshiro. They worked their way toward the rear of the ship. Midway, in the tube aisle, the capsule was nearly clear of the tube. Toshiro floated among globs of blood near the ceiling. Lucas pushed the legs out of the way so he could look through the small window.

"She's here," he called to Ferguson.

"Is it still airtight?"

Lucas checked the gauge.

"Yes. A small amount of air left."

"Is she okay?"

"I can't tell," Lucas said with concern. "She's asleep or unconscious."

Ferguson cursed under his breath. He shouldn't have let her come. He shouldn't have obeyed her order. He blamed Lucas and the others for taking so long to arrive, even while admitting that wasn't the least bit fair. More, he blamed Toshiro and his ships for not leaving them alone, and fate for its overall unfairness. All in a few blistering words.

"Let's get her out of here," he said aloud.

It is time to return, Laicy. They are here.

"I am not going back."

What do you mean?

"I want to stay here for a time. There is peace here. No demands. You can come for me sometime, and I will be one of the companions. But not now."

You cannot do that. The Glaive needs you. Your friends need you.

"For what? I have done the most important thing for the Glaive. It is well on its way, operating smoothly. As for my friends, they will get along without me too."

If they do not want to?

"They will learn."

And the Glaive. Do you think it would survive, much less grow stronger, without your leadership? Its purpose, its sense of direction, must be firmly set now. A successor must be chosen and trained. The process has begun but no permanent decisions on basic management have been made.

"You can do that. With Crowell. Or Lucas. Any of the others. I want to disappear, to be dead, for a while. No demands. No decisions. No killing. Friend or enemy.

"You said yourself, a little while ago, that I was going about killing in a cold manner."

The Glaive has enough martyrs. They died at Crowell's. Including your father. The last thing we need is a martyr who chooses to die because she is tired.

"Ensi . . ."

Those people died because they believed in the Glaive, in you. Two of them risk their lives right here trying to save you. If you leave now, the deaths and work of so many will have been for nothing. I will not come back for you.

Lucas and Ferguson will take your body away soon. I am going with them.

"You just don't understand. You don't know . . ."

He was gone.

They struggled to free the capsule from the tube, then the aisle. As they moved through the silent ship, they wondered aloud if it could be moved through the hole by which they had entered. Ferguson called ahead, telling his crew to get ready to enlarge it with torches just in case.

No matter how one looked at it, there was not much time left. The air in the capsule was extremely low. Iroshi was not conscious, possibly because of some injury caused by the crash or by Toshiro.

Lucas wondered why Ensi was not communicating with him. Janue probed for the other companion, but was unable to contact him.

Others of the crews in the three racers and the warriors offered to come help. There just wasn't enough room for any more, and the two of them struggled alone, sweat rolling down their faces and sides in spite of the coolers inside the suits. Twisted pieces of metal and plastic barred the way here and there and had to be wrenched forward or bent back. It seemed to take forever, but they finally reached the opening.

The capsule would fit through if they forced it, but there was too much danger of a puncture. Two of the crew worked rapidly outside, removing the worst pieces of the ragged edge.

As the work progressed, Ferguson looked in at Iroshi once more.

"Any change?" Lucas asked.

"None."

Lucas checked the gauges.

"About the same here."

They waited, until those outside motioned for them to try it. Gently, they pushed the capsule forward. If they kept it fairly straight, it would make it. The two outside steadied what might possibly be a coffin. Lucas guided it from the side while Ferguson pushed from behind.

Nearly clear, Lucas came too close to a jagged piece jutting inward. It caught the right leg of his suit, cutting through to his leg. Oxygen dissipated in a cloud into the airlessness. In horror, Lucas froze, unable to react to a totally alien emergency.

Without a word one of the unknown crewmen came to him with a tube of patch paste and squeezed some out along the rip. The yellow substance bubbled as it set up. His savior patted Lucas on the shoulder, letting him know it was all right; Lucas, after a quick check of the gauge on his sleeve, gave a thumbs-up

Although shaken, Lucas resumed his position. The capsule was free of the racer, and they moved swiftly to the airlock on the waiting vessel. Normally the capsule would have been pushed into the tube, but the airlock would be faster. Everyone was set. They moved through quickly. The men removed only their helmets as they pushed their cargo into the aisle. Ferguson keyed in the open command, but nothing happened.

"Jammed," someone gritted.

But they were ready with tools to pry it open. At the same time one of the men worked on making a hole at the foot of the capsule away from the lid.

They waited, sweating and swearing quietly; Lucas noted the crewman who saved him outside and made a note to thank her later.

With a loud click, the top broke free. Many hands raised it. Someone put an oxygen mask over Iroshi's face. Ferguson checked the carotid pulse. He pulled up her arm, checked the pulse in the wrist. As he waited, as they waited, his expression did not change.

He raised his head. His eyes met those of Lucas, who could see tears glistening in the captain's, and he turned away, knowing sorrow greater than ever before.

"She can't be dead," a voice quavered.

"She moved!" someone else said.

Everyone looked. Nothing. Then a slight moan. A quivering eyelid.

"She's all right," Lucas shouted.

"She's alive," Ferguson corrected.

• • •

"Are you certain you don't want to see the doctor on Amber?"

Iroshi reclined on the bed in her cabin. Captain Ferguson sat in the chair near the door.

"No, thank you, Captain. I am feeling fine and anxious to get home."

"That won't be for another four weeks."

She nodded.

"If you need anything, just holler." He rose to leave.

"Thank you, again, Captain."

He bowed and left.

"You were right, Ensi. They do seem very happy to have me with them again."

They are. You and the Glaive give purpose to their lives.

"In whatever time I have left, will I be able to accomplish all of it? Will the Glaive be where we envision it?"

All I really know is that if we learn from everything that happens, we will always be moving forward. How much can be achieved in one lifetime? It is hard to say.

"One thing is certain."

What is that?

"The legend of Iroshi keeps growing."

There does seem to be a strong element of awe among the crew.

"Lucas is acting differently too. We must explain revay to him soon."

She sat quietly for a moment, then rose to unsheathe her katana and begin practice.

"It's Mitchell I worry about."

Do you think it may be too much for him? This new myth?

"Yes."

Not to worry. He loves you and will accept you with or without the legend. He always has, even though he will never fully understand what you and the Glaive are all about.

You and I are part and parcel of the same thing. Martial arts. Meditation. The Glaive. All that keeps us of one mind at times. Mitchell is your balance. He keeps you, us, from floating off into the haze of the void.

Iroshi raised the sword. Just before she centered her concentration, she smiled. Knowing Mitchell waited for her was one thing that made coming back worthwhile.

The blade arced overhead, and she passed into the void.